SEVEN MEN
AND TWO OTHERS

MAX BEERBOHM was born in 1872 and educated at Charterhouse and Merton College, Oxford. William Rothenstein – who had been impressed by his work as a cartoonist – introduced him to literary and artistic London in 1893: he became acquainted with Aubrey Beardsley and Oscar Wilde, contributed to the *Yellow Book*, succeeded Bernard Shaw as dramatic critic of the *Saturday Review*, and published *The Works of Max Beerbohm* – a collection of essays – in 1896. In 1910 he married the American actress Florence Kahn: they settled in Rapallo on the Italian Riviera, which was to remain Max Beerbohm's home for the rest of his life. Max Beerbohm was knighted in 1939; three years later he was awarded an honorary D. Litt. by Oxford and made an honorary fellow of his old college. He died in 1956. Apart from *Seven Men* (1919), his best known books include *The Happy Hypocrite* (1897), *Zuleika Dobson* (1911), and *A Christmas Garland* (1912).

LORD DAVID CECIL was the Goldsmiths' Professor of English Literature at Oxford from 1948 to 1969. *Max* – his biography of Max Beerbohm – was published in 1964; his other books include *The Stricken Deer*, *The Young Melbourne*, *Lord M.*, *Library Looking-glass*, *The Cecils of Hatfield House*, and *A Portrait of Jane Austen*.

THE WORLD'S CLASSICS

MAX BEERBOHM

Seven Men
and Two Others

With an Introduction by
LORD DAVID CECIL, C.H.

Oxford New York Toronto Melbourne
OXFORD UNIVERSITY PRESS
1980

Oxford University Press, Walton Street, Oxford OX2 6DP
OXFORD   LONDON   GLASGOW
NEW YORK   TORONTO   MELBOURNE   WELLINGTON
KUALA LUMPUR   SINGAPORE   JAKARTA   HONG KONG   TOKYO
DELHI   BOMBAY   CALCUTTA   MADRAS   KARACHI
NAIROBI   DAR ES SALAAM   CAPE TOWN

Seven Men was first published in 1919 by William Heinemann Ltd
The 'Two Others' were added to the edition of 1950
which was included in The World's Classics *in 1966 and*
first issued as a paperback World's Classic *in 1980*
Introduction © Oxford University Press 1966

British Library Cataloguing in Publication Data
Beerbohm, Sir Max
Seven men and two others.
I. Title
823'.9'1FS   PR6003.E4S| 79-42711
ISBN 0-19-281512-1

Printed in Great Britain by
Hazell Watson & Viney Ltd,
Aylesbury, Bucks

CONTENTS

NOTE

[TO THE 1950 EDITION]

My memories of the 'two others' appeared only
in *A Variety of Things*, one of the volumes in a
limited edition of my books; and it has seemed
to me that they would now come not amiss in
this new edition of *Seven Men*. Hence their
intrusion.

M.B., 1949.

INTRODUCTION

ANY judgement of value in a literary matter is always risky. But why not take a risk sometimes? Let me say then that, for me at any rate, *Seven Men and Two Others* is the finest expression of the comic spirit produced by any English writer during this century. Though tone and style give it unity, it is in fact made up of six self-dependent studies, written at intervals over a period of years. Max wrote 'Enoch Soames' and 'James Pethel' at Rapallo in 1914; while 'Hilary Maltby and Stephen Braxton', 'A. V. Laider', and 'Savonarola Brown' were composed during the years 1915–17 when he was living at Far Oakridge, in a cottage lent him by his friend William Rothenstein. All these were published together in 1919 under the title *Seven Men*. In 1927, back in Italy, he wrote 'Felix Argallo and Walter Ledgett' which first appeared in the *London Mercury*. It is an essay in the same vein as the others; and when in 1950 *Seven Men* was reprinted, Max added 'Argallo and Ledgett' to it and changed the title to *Seven Men and Two Others*.

In it, for the first and only time, he unites two characteristic strains in his art. *Seven Men* differs from Max's previous stories in the fact that he brings himself openly into it. He had always done this in his essays. It is the presence of his personality, demure, ironic, detached, observant, that gives them their individual charm. He does not appear in the earlier stories. But in *Seven Men* the essayist has become a character in the drama. The Seventh Man is Max himself who both narrates the tale and takes part in the action. In 'Maltby and Braxton' he actually makes a double appearance; for poor little Maltby relating his misfortunes to Max is himself a caricature of his creator; in Maltby, Max is laughing at his own social vanities and embarrassments. The character of A. V. Laider, too, reflects both Max's love of a hoax and his tendency to let things slide in order to avoid trouble.

Further, each tale has been inspired by a phase in Max's life. 'Enoch Soames' is about literary London of the nineties and Max's entry into it. 'Maltby and Braxton' is suggested by his excursions into Edwardian high-life; Keeb Hall is Taplow Court, the Duchess of Hertfordshire is Lady Desborough, and Lady Rodfitten is Lady Londonderry. These two stories also include real people undisguised, William Rothenstein and Mr. Balfour. Of the other stories, 'Savonarola Brown' was inspired by Max's life as dramatic critic. 'Laider' by the solitary visits he used to pay to the English seaside in winter, and 'Argallo and Ledgett' by his experience of the literary world. Altogether *Seven Men* is the most autobiographical of Max's works.

Not very autobiographical, however! Even when it is not too fantastic, it is too amusing. He is careful to keep his entertainment continuously entertaining. The spirit of comedy pervades its every page. And at her purest: Max's fantasy never grows too dreamy to observe and to smile. Again though he makes ruthless fun of human weakness, he never seems out of temper. Any touch of bitterness, he realized, would destroy the amenity of his entertainment. Nor does he go in for the grim joke. Three of his heroes die: but the deaths of Argallo and Brown are too uproariously absurd to be grim; while Pethel's death only occurs in a postscript where it is reported to Max many years after he had last seen him. Moreover it is as little distressing a death as could possibly be.

It might be thought that to keep the atmosphere so consistently light-hearted would mean monotony. But Max's humour is very varied. Here it is that he outdistances all his competitors. Others may rival him as a satirist, parodist, fantasist, humorous observer. In *Seven Men* his comic genius shines out unsurpassed in all these forms; and others too. Each phase enhances the other. 'Enoch Soames' for instance is rollickingly fantastic and also the most illuminating record we have of the Yellow Book epoch. Maltby's ghostly misadventures at Keeb Hall are combined— I can vouch for it—with the most accurate picture of an Edwardian house party in our literature. Nor, granted the preposterous hypotheses on which they are founded, are Max's fantasies irrational. Note how neatly he explains at the end of the story why Soames, a real man, will yet be mistaken in the future for a character in fiction.

Max's parody too gains its effect because it is so near to the real thing. Soames's poems are only just more absurd than the typical Yellow Book poem of the time. In 'Argallo and Ledgett' the notes from Meredith and Patmore evoke the manner and spirit

of each author exactly. 'Savonarola Brown' achieves
a greater feat. Intended no doubt to parody the
pseudo-Shakespeare plays of Max's own time, it
turns into a parody of Shakespeare himself. It has
been said that Shakespeare cannot be parodied. Max
does it. The Fool is splendidly close to Feste.

> If he be right astronomically, Mistress, then is he the
> greater dunce in respect of true learning, the which goes
> by the globe. Argal, 'twere better he widened his wind-pipe.
>
> (*sings*)
>
> Fly home, sweet self,
> Nothing's for weeping,
> Hemp was not made
> For lovers' keeping,
> Lovers' keeping,
> Cheerly, cheerly, fly away.

Some would say that Max was most amusing as
a parodist. For myself I enjoy him most as the
amused observer of human weaknesses, more especially his own; as here, at his first encounter with
Pethel the successful gambler for high stakes. Envy
has made Max a little hostile.

> We were introduced. He spoke to me with some *empresse-
> ment*, saying he was a 'very great admirer' of my work.
> I no longer disliked him. Grierson, armed with counters,
> had now darted away to secure a place that had just been
> vacated. Pethel, with a wave of his hand towards the tables,
> said, 'I suppose you never condescend to this sort of thing?'
> 'Well——' I smiled indulgently.
> 'Awful waste of time,' he admitted.
> I glanced down at the splendid mess of counters and gold
> and notes that were now becoming, under the swift fingers
> of the little man at the bureau, an orderly array. I did not

say aloud that it pleased me to be, and to be seen, talking, on terms of equality, to a man who had won so much. I did not say how wonderful it seemed to me that he, whom I had watched just now with awe and with aversion, had all the while been a great admirer of my work. I did but say (again indulgently) that I supposed baccarat to be as good a way of wasting time as another.

What penetration this shows, and how deftly, gracefully, lightly it is expressed. Max's art is so exquisite, his sense of form and words so felicitous as to make his comedy not only varied and entertaining but also a thing of beauty. In this again, he is unrivalled. No!—I cannot repent of my risky statement. *Seven Men* is surely the finest expression of the comic spirit produced by any English writer during this century.

DAVID CECIL

ENOCH SOAMES

ENOCH SOAMES

1912

WHEN a book about the literature of the eighteen-nineties was given by Mr. Holbrook Jackson to the world, I looked eagerly in the index for SOAMES, ENOCH. I had feared he would not be there. He was not there. But everybody else was. Many writers whom I had quite forgotten, or remembered but faintly, lived again for me, they and their work, in Mr. Holbrook Jackson's pages. The book was as thorough as it was brilliantly written. And thus the omission found by me was an all the deadlier record of poor Soames' failure to impress himself on his decade.

I daresay I am the only person who noticed the omission. Soames had failed so piteously as all that! Nor is there a counterpoise in the thought that if he had had some measure of success he might have passed, like those others, out of my mind, to return only at the historian's beck. It is true that had his gifts, such as they were, been acknowledged in his lifetime, he would never have made the bargain I saw him make—that strange bargain whose results have kept him always in the foreground of my memory. But it is from those very results that the full piteousness of him glares out.

Not my compassion, however, impels me to write of him. For his sake, poor fellow, I should be inclined to keep my pen out of the ink. It is ill to deride the dead. And how can I write about Enoch Soames without making him ridiculous? Or rather, how am I to hush up the horrid fact that he *was* ridiculous? I shall not be able to do that. Yet, sooner or later, write about him I must. You will see, in due course, that I have no option. And I may as well get the thing done now.

In the Summer Term of '93 a bolt from the blue flashed down on Oxford. It drove deep, it hurtlingly embedded itself in the soil. Dons and undergraduates stood around, rather pale, discussing nothing but it. Whence came it, this meteorite? From Paris. Its name? Will Rothenstein. Its aim? To do a series of twenty-four portraits in lithograph. These were to be published from the Bodley Head, London. The matter was urgent. Already the Warden of A, and the Master of B, and the Regius Professor of C, had meekly 'sat.' Dignified and doddering old men, who had never consented to sit to any one, could not withstand this dynamic little stranger. He did not sue: he invited; he did not invite: he commanded. He was twenty-one years old. He wore spectacles that flashed more than any other pair ever seen. He was a wit. He was brimful of ideas. He knew Whistler. He knew Edmond de Goncourt. He knew every one in Paris. He knew them all by heart. He was Paris in Oxford. It was whispered that, so soon as he had polished off his selection of dons, he was going to include a few undergraduates. It was a proud day for me when I— I—was included. I liked Rothenstein not less than I feared him; and there arose between us a friendship that has grown ever warmer, and been more and more valued by me, with every passing year.

At the end of Term he settled in—or rather, meteoritically into—London. It was to him I owed my first knowledge of that forever enchanting little world-in-itself, Chelsea, and my first acquaintance with Walter Sickert and other august elders who dwelt there. It was Rothenstein that took me to see, in Cambridge Street, Pimlico, a young man whose drawings were already famous among the few— Aubrey Beardsley, by name. With Rothenstein I paid my first visit to the Bodley Head. By him I was inducted into another haunt of intellect and daring, the domino room of the Café Royal.

There, on that October evening—there, in that exuberant vista of gilding and crimson velvet set amidst all those opposing mirrors and upholding caryatids, with fumes of tobacco ever rising to the painted and pagan ceiling, and with the hum of presumably cynical conversation broken into so sharply now and again by the clatter of dominoes shuffled on marble tables, I drew a deep breath, and 'This indeed,' said I to myself, 'is life!'

It was the hour before dinner. We drank vermouth. Those who knew Rothenstein were pointing him out to those who knew him only by name. Men were constantly coming in through the swing-doors and wandering slowly up and down in search of vacant tables, or of tables occupied by friends. One of these rovers interested me because I was sure he wanted to catch Rothenstein's eye. He had twice passed our table, with a hesitating look; but Rothenstein, in the thick of a disquisition on Puvis de Chavannes, had not seen him. He was a stooping, shambling person, rather tall, very pale, with longish and brownish hair. He had a thin vague beard—or rather, he had a chin on which a large number of hairs weakly curled and clustered to cover its retreat. He was an odd-looking person; but in the 'nineties odd apparitions were more frequent, I think, than they are now. The young writers of that era—and I was sure this man was a writer—strove earnestly to be distinct in aspect. This man had striven unsuccessfully. He wore a soft black hat of clerical kind but of Bohemian intention, and a grey waterproof cape which, perhaps because it was waterproof, failed to be romantic. I decided that 'dim' was the *mot juste* for him. I had already essayed to write, and was immensely keen on the *mot juste*, that Holy Grail of the period.

The dim man was now again approaching our table, and this time he made up his mind to pause in front of it. 'You don't remember me,' he said in a toneless voice.

Rothenstein brightly focussed him. 'Yes, I do,' he replied after a moment, with pride rather than effusion—pride in a retentive memory. 'Edwin Soames.'

'Enoch Soames,' said Enoch.

'Enoch Soames,' repeated Rothenstein in a tone implying that it was enough to have hit on the surname. 'We met in Paris two or three times when you were living there. We met at the Café Groche.'

'And I came to your studio once.'

'Oh yes; I was sorry I was out.'

'But you were in. You showed me some of your

paintings, you know. . . . I hear you're in Chelsea now.'

'Yes.'

I almost wondered that Mr. Soames did not, after this monosyllable, pass along. He stood patiently there, rather like a dumb animal, rather like a donkey looking over a gate. A sad figure, his. It occurred to me that 'hungry' was perhaps the *mot juste* for him; but—hungry for what? He looked as if he had little appetite for anything. I was sorry for him; and Rothenstein, though he had not invited him to Chelsea, did ask him to sit down and have something to drink.

Seated, he was more self-assertive. He flung back the wings of his cape with a gesture which—had not those wings been waterproof—might have seemed to hurl defiance at things in general. And he ordered an absinthe. '*Je me tiens toujours fidèle*,' he told Rothenstein, '*à la sorcière glauque*.'

'It is bad for you,' said Rothenstein drily.

'Nothing is bad for one,' answered Soames. '*Dans ce monde il n'y a ni de bien ni de mal*.'

'Nothing good and nothing bad? How do you mean?'

'I explained it all in the preface to "Negations."'

'"Negations"?'

'Yes; I gave you a copy of it.'

'Oh yes, of course. But did you explain—for instance—that there was no such thing as bad or good grammar?'

'N-no,' said Soames. 'Of course in Art there is the good and the evil. But in Life—no.' He was rolling a cigarette. He had weak white hands, not well washed, and with finger-tips much stained by nicotine. 'In Life there are illusions of good and evil, but'—his voice trailed away to a murmur in which the words 'vieux jeu' and 'rococo' were faintly audible. I think he felt he was not doing himself justice, and feared that Rothenstein was going to point out fallacies. Anyway, he cleared his throat and said '*Parlons d'autre chose.*'

It occurs to you that he was a fool? It didn't to me. I was young, and had not the clarity of judgment that Rothenstein already had. Soames was quite five or six years older than either of us. Also, he had written a book.

It was wonderful to have written a book.

If Rothenstein had not been there, I should have revered Soames. Even as it was, I respected him. And I was very near indeed to reverence when he said he had another book coming out soon. I asked if I might ask what kind of book it was to be.

'My poems,' he answered. Rothenstein asked if this was to be the title of the book. The poet meditated on this suggestion, but said he rather thought of giving the book no title at all. 'If a book is good in itself——' he murmured, waving his cigarette.

Rothenstein objected that absence of title might be bad for the sale of a book. 'If,' he urged, 'I went into a bookseller's and said simply "Have you got?" or "Have you a copy of?" how would they know what I wanted?'

'Oh, of course I should have my name on the cover,' Soames answered earnestly. 'And I rather want,' he added, looking hard at Rothenstein, 'to have a drawing of myself as frontispiece.' Rothenstein admitted that this was a capital idea, and mentioned that he was going into the country and would be there for some time. He then looked at his watch, exclaimed at the hour, paid the waiter, and went away with me to dinner. Soames remained at his post of fidelity to the glaucous witch.

'Why were you so determined not to draw him?' I asked.

'Draw him? Him? How can one draw a man who doesn't exist?'

'He is dim,' I admitted. But my *mot juste* fell flat. Rothenstein repeated that Soames was non-existent.

Still, Soames had written a book. I asked if Rothenstein had read 'Negations.' He said he had looked into it, 'but,' he added crisply, 'I don't profess to know anything about writing.' A reservation very characteristic of the period! Painters would not then allow that any one outside their own order had a right to any opinion about painting. This law (graven on the tablets brought down by Whistler from the summit of Fujiyama) imposed certain limitations. If other arts than painting were not utterly unintelligible to all but the men who practised them, the law tottered—the Monroe Doctrine, as it were, did not hold good. Therefore no painter would offer an opinion of a book without warning you at any rate that his opinion was worthless. No one is a better judge of literature than Rothenstein; but it wouldn't have done to tell him so in those days; and I knew that I must form an unaided judgment on 'Negations.'

Not to buy a book of which I had met the author face to face would have been for me in those days an impossible act of self-denial. When I returned to Oxford for the Christmas Term I had duly secured 'Negations.' I used to keep it lying carelessly on the table in my room, and whenever a friend took it up and asked what it was about I would say 'Oh, it's rather a remarkable book. It's by a man whom I know.' Just 'what it was about' I never was able to say. Head or tail was just what I hadn't made of that slim green volume. I found in the preface no clue to the exiguous labyrinth of contents, and in that labyrinth nothing to explain the preface.

Lean near to life. Lean very near—nearer.

Life is web, and therein nor warp nor woof is, but web only.

It is for this I am Catholick in church and in thought, yet do let swift Mood weave there what the shuttle of Mood wills.

These were the opening phrases of the preface, but those which followed were less easy to understand. Then came 'Stark: A *Conte*', about a midinette who, so far as I could gather, murdered, or was about to murder, a mannequin. It seemed to me like a story by Catulle Mendès in which the translator had either skipped or cut out every alternate sentence. Next, a dialogue between Pan and St. Ursula—lacking, I rather felt, in 'snap.' Next, some aphorisms (entitled ἀφορίσματα). Throughout, in fact, there was a great variety of form; and the forms had evidently been wrought with much care. It was rather the substance that eluded me. Was there, I wondered, any substance at all? It did now occur to me: suppose Enoch Soames was a fool! Up cropped a rival hypothesis: suppose *I* was! I inclined to give Soames the benefit of the doubt. I had read 'L'Après-midi d'un Faune' without extracting a glimmer of meaning. Yet Mallarmé—of course—was a Master. How was I to know that Soames wasn't another? There was a sort of music in his prose, not indeed arresting, but perhaps, I thought, haunting, and laden perhaps with meanings as deep as Mallarmé's own. I awaited his poems with an open mind.

And I looked forward to them with positive impatience after I had had a second meeting with him. This was on an evening in January. Going into the aforesaid domino room, I passed a table at which sat a pale man with an open book before him. He looked from his book to me, and I looked back over my shoulder with a vague sense that I ought to have recognised him. I returned to pay my respects. After exchanging a few words, I said with a glance to the open book, 'I see I am interrupting you,' and was about to pass on, but 'I prefer,' Soames replied in his toneless voice, 'to be interrupted,' and I obeyed his gesture that I should sit down.

I asked him if he often read here. 'Yes; things of this kind I read here,' he answered, indicating the title of his book—'The Poems of Shelley.'

'Anything that you really'—and I was going to say 'admire?' But I cautiously left my sentence unfinished, and was glad that I had done so, for he said, with unwonted emphasis, 'Anything second-rate.'

I had read little of Shelley, but 'Of course,' I murmured, 'he's very uneven.'

'I should have thought evenness was just what was
wrong with him. A deadly evenness. That's why
I read him here. The noise of this place breaks the
rhythm. He's tolerable here.' Soames took up the
book and glanced through the pages. He laughed.
Soames' laugh was a short, single and mirthless
sound from the throat, unaccompanied by any movement of the face or brightening of the eyes. 'What
a period!' he uttered, laying the book down. And
'What a country!' he added.

I asked rather nervously if he didn't think Keats
had more or less held his own against the drawbacks
of time and place. He admitted that there were
'passages in Keats,' but did not specify them. Of
'the older men,' as he called them, he seemed to like
only Milton. 'Milton,' he said, 'wasn't sentimental.'
Also, 'Milton had a dark insight.' And again, 'I can
always read Milton in the reading-room.'

'The reading-room?'

'Of the British Museum. I go there every day.'

'You do? I've only been there once. I'm afraid I
found it rather a depressing place. It—it seemed to
sap one's vitality.'

'It does. That's why I go there. The lower one's
vitality, the more sensitive one is to great art. I
live near the Museum. I have rooms in Dyott
Street.'

'And you go round to the reading-room to read
Milton?'

'Usually Milton.' He looked at me. 'It was Milton,'

he certificatively added, 'who converted me to Diabolism.'

'Diabolism? Oh yes? Really?' said I, with that vague discomfort and that intense desire to be polite which one feels when a man speaks of his own religion. 'You—worship the Devil?'

Soames shook his head. 'It's not exactly worship,' he qualified, sipping his absinthe. 'It's more a matter of trusting and encouraging.'

'Ah, yes. . . . But I had rather gathered from the preface to "Negations" that you were a—a Catholic.'

'*Je l'étais à cette époque.* Perhaps I still am. Yes, I'm a Catholic Diabolist.'

This profession he made in an almost cursory tone. I could see that what was upmost in his mind was the fact that I had read 'Negations.' His pale eyes had for the first time gleamed. I felt as one who is about to be examined, *viva voce*, on the very subject in which he is shakiest. I hastily asked him how soon his poems were to be published. 'Next week,' he told me.

'And are they to be published without a title?'

'No. I found a title, at last. But I shan't tell you what it is,' as though I had been so impertinent as to inquire. 'I am not sure that it wholly satisfies me. But it is the best I can find. It does suggest something of the quality of the poems. . . . Strange growths, natural and wild; yet exquisite,' he added, 'and many-hued, and full of poisons.'

I asked him what he thought of Baudelaire. He uttered the snort that was his laugh, and 'Baudelaire,' he said, 'was a *bourgeois malgré lui*.' France

had had only one poet: Villon; 'and two-thirds of
Villon were sheer journalism.' Verlaine was 'an
épicier malgré lui.' Altogether, rather to my surprise,
he rated French literature lower than English. There
were 'passages' in Villiers de l'Isle-Adam. But 'I,'
he summed up, 'owe nothing to France.' He nodded
at me. 'You'll see,' he predicted.

I did not, when the time came, quite see that. I
thought the author of 'Fungoids' did—unconsciously, no doubt—owe something to the young
Parisian décadents, or to the young English ones who
owed something to *them*. I still think so. The little
book—bought by me in Oxford—lies before me as I
write. Its pale grey buckram cover and silver letter-
ing have not worn well. Nor have its contents.
Through these, with a melancholy interest, I have
again been looking. They are not much. But at the
time of their publication I had a vague suspicion that
they *might* be. I suppose it is my capacity for faith,
not poor Soames' work, that is weaker than it once
was. . . .

To a Young Woman

> *Thou art, who hast not been!*
>   Pale tunes irresolute
>   And traceries of old sounds
>   Blown from a rotted flute
> Mingle with noise of cymbals rouged with rust,
> Nor not strange forms and epicene
>   Lie bleeding in the dust,
>   Being wounded with wounds.

> For this it is
> That is thy counterpart
> Of age-long mockeries
> *Thou hast not been nor art!*

There seemed to me a certain inconsistency as between the first and last lines of this. I tried, with bent brows, to resolve the discord. But I did not take my failure as wholly incompatible with a meaning in Soames' mind. Might it not rather indicate the depth of his meaning? As for the craftsmanship, 'rouged with rust' seemed to me a fine stroke, and 'nor not' instead of 'and' had a curious felicity. I wondered who the Young Woman was, and what she had made of it all. I sadly suspect that Soames could not have made more of it than she. Yet, even now, if one doesn't try to make any sense at all of the poem, and reads it just for the sound, there is a certain grace of cadence. Soames was an artist—in so far as he was anything, poor fellow!

It seemed to me, when first I read 'Fungoids,' that, oddly enough, the Diabolistic side of him was the best. Diabolism seemed to be a cheerful, even a wholesome, influence in his life.

NOCTURNE

> Round and round the shutter'd Square
> I stroll'd with the Devil's arm in mine.
> No sound but the scrape of his hoofs was there
> And the ring of his laughter and mine.
> We had drunk black wine.

I scream'd 'I will race you, Master!'
'What matter,' he shriek'd, 'to-night
Which of us runs the faster?
There is nothing to fear to-night
  In the foul moon's light!'

Then I look'd him in the eyes,
And I laugh'd full shrill at the lie he told
And the gnawing fear he would fain disguise.
It was true, what I'd time and again been told:
  He was old—old.

There was, I felt, quite a swing about that first stanza—a joyous and rollicking note of comradeship. The second was slightly hysterical perhaps. But I liked the third: it was so bracingly unorthodox, even according to the tenets of Soames' peculiar sect in the faith. Not much 'trusting and encouraging' here! Soames triumphantly exposing the Devil as a liar, and laughing 'full shrill,' cut a quite heartening figure, I thought—then! Now, in the light of what befell, none of his poems depresses me so much as 'Nocturne.'

I looked out for what the metropolitan reviewers would have to say. They seemed to fall into two classes: those who had little to say and those who had nothing. The second class was the larger, and the words of the first were cold; insomuch that

Strikes a note of modernity throughout. . . . These tripping numbers.—*Preston Telegraph.*

was the sole lure offered in advertisements by Soames' publisher. I had hoped that when next I met the poet I could congratulate him on having made a stir; for I fancied he was not so sure of his intrinsic greatness as he seemed. I was but able to say, rather coarsely, when next I did see him, that I hoped 'Fungoids' was 'selling splendidly.' He looked at me across his glass of absinthe and asked if I had bought a copy. His publisher had told him that three had been sold. I laughed, as at a jest.

'You don't suppose I *care*, do you?' he said, with something like a snarl. I disclaimed the notion. He added that he was not a tradesman. I said mildly that I wasn't, either, and murmured that an artist who gave truly new and great things to the world had always to wait long for recognition. He said he cared not a sou for recognition. I agreed that the act of creation was its own reward.

His moroseness might have alienated me if I had regarded myself as a nobody. But ah! hadn't both John Lane and Aubrey Beardsley suggested that I should write an essay for the great new venture that was afoot—'The Yellow Book'? And hadn't Henry Harland, as editor, accepted my essay? And wasn't it to be in the very first number? At Oxford I was still *in statu pupillari*. In London I regarded myself as very much indeed a graduate now—one whom no Soames could ruffle. Partly to show off, partly in sheer good-will, I told Soames he ought to contribute to 'The Yellow Book.' He uttered from the throat a sound of scorn for that publication.

Nevertheless, I did, a day or two later, tentatively ask Harland if he knew anything of the work of a man called Enoch Soames. Harland paused in the midst of his characteristic stride around the room, threw up his hands towards the ceiling, and groaned aloud: he had often met 'that absurd creature' in Paris, and this very morning had received some poems in manuscript from him.

'Has he *no* talent?' he asked.

'He has an income. He's all right.' Harland was the most joyous of men and most generous of critics, and he hated to talk of anything about which he couldn't be enthusiastic. So I dropped the subject of Soames. The news that Soames had an income did take the edge off solicitude. I learned afterwards that he was the son of an unsuccessful and deceased bookseller in Preston, but had inherited an annuity of £300 from a married aunt, and had no surviving relatives of any kind. Materially, then, he was 'all right.' But there was still a spiritual pathos about him, sharpened for me now by the possibility that even the praises of 'The Preston Telegraph' might not have been forthcoming had he not been the son of a Preston man. He had a sort of weak doggedness which I could not but admire. Neither he nor his work received the slightest encouragement; but he persisted in behaving as a personage: always he kept his dingy little flag flying. Wherever congregated the *jeunes féroces* of the arts, in whatever Soho restaurant they had just discovered, in whatever music-hall they were most frequenting, there was Soames in the midst of them, or rather on the fringe of them, a dim but inevitable figure. He never sought to propitiate his fellow-writers, never bated a jot of his arrogance about his own work or of his contempt for theirs. To

the painters he was respectful, even humble; but for
the poets and prosaists of 'The Yellow Book,' and
later of 'The Savoy,' he had never a word but of
scorn. He wasn't resented. It didn't occur to anybody that he or his Catholic Diabolism mattered.
When, in the autumn of '96, he brought out (at his
own expense, this time) a third book, his last book,
nobody said a word for or against it. I meant, but forgot, to buy it. I never saw it, and am ashamed to say
I don't even remember what it was called. But I did,
at the time of its publication, say to Rothenstein that
I thought poor old Soames was really a rather tragic
figure, and that I believed he would literally die for
want of recognition. Rothenstein scoffed. He said I
was trying to get credit for a kind heart which I didn't
possess; and perhaps this was so. But at the private
view of the New English Art Club, a few weeks later,
I beheld a pastel portrait of 'Enoch Soames, Esq.'
It was very like him, and very like Rothenstein to have
done it. Soames was standing near it, in his soft hat
and his waterproof cape, all through the afternoon.
Anybody who knew him would have recognised the
portrait at a glance, but nobody who didn't know him
would have recognised the portrait from its by-
stander: it 'existed' so much more than he; it was
bound to. Also, it had not that expression of faint
happiness which on this day was discernible, yes, in
Soames' countenance. Fame had breathed on him.
Twice again in the course of the month I went to the
New English, and on both occasions Soames himself
was on view there. Looking back, I regard the close
of that exhibition as having been virtually the close of

his career. He had felt the breath of Fame against his
cheek—so late, for such a little while; and at its with-
drawal he gave in, gave up, gave out. He, who had
never looked strong or well, looked ghastly now—
a shadow of the shade he had once been. He still
frequented the domino room, but, having lost all
wish to excite curiosity, he no longer read books
there. 'You read only at the Museum now?' asked
I, with attempted cheerfulness. He said he never
went there now. 'No absinthe there,' he muttered.
It was the sort of thing that in the old days he would
have said for effect; but it carried conviction now.
Absinthe, erst but a point in the 'personality' he had
striven so hard to build up, was solace and necessity
now. He no longer called it 'la sorcière glauque.' He
had shed away all his French phrases. He had become a plain, unvarnished, Preston man.

Failure, if it be a plain, unvarnished, complete
failure, and even though it be a squalid failure, has
always a certain dignity. I avoided Soames because
he made me feel rather vulgar. John Lane had
published, by this time, two little books of mine, and
they had had a pleasant little success of esteem. I was
a—slight but definite—'personality.' Frank Harris
had engaged me to kick up my heels in *The Saturday
Review*, Alfred Harmsworth was letting me do like-
wise in *The Daily Mail*. I was just what Soames
wasn't. And he shamed my gloss. Had I known that
he really and firmly believed in the greatness of what
he as an artist had achieved, I might not have
shunned him. No man who hasn't lost his vanity can
be held to have altogether failed. Soames' dignity was

an illusion of mine. One day in the first week of June,
1897, that illusion went. But on the evening of that
day Soames went too.

I had been out most of the morning, and, as it was
too late to reach home in time for luncheon, I sought
'the Vingtième.' This little place—Restaurant du
Vingtième Siècle, to give it its full title—had been
discovered in '96 by the poets and prosaists, but had
now been more or less abandoned in favour of some
later find. I don't think it lived long enough to justify
its name; but at that time there it still was, in Greek
Street, a few doors from Soho Square, and almost
opposite to that house where, in the first years of the
century, a little girl, and with her a boy named De
Quincey, made nightly encampment in darkness and
hunger among dust and rats and old legal parch-
ments. The Vingtième was but a small whitewashed
room, leading out into the street at one end and into
a kitchen at the other. The proprietor and cook was
a Frenchman, known to us as Monsieur Vingtième;
the waiters were his two daughters, Rose and Berthe;
and the food, according to faith, was good. The
tables were so narrow, and were set so close together,
that there was space for twelve of them, six jutting
from either wall.

Only the two nearest to the door, as I went in,
were occupied. On one side sat a tall, flashy, rather
Mephistophelian man whom I had seen from time
to time in the domino room and elsewhere. On the
other side sat Soames. They made a queer contrast
in that sunlit room—Soames sitting haggard in that
hat and cape which nowhere at any season had I seen

him doff, and this other, this keenly vital man, at
sight of whom I more than ever wondered whether
he were a diamond merchant, a conjurer, or the head
of a private detective agency. I was sure Soames
didn't want my company; but I asked, as it would
have seemed brutal not to, whether I might join him,
and took the chair opposite to his. He was smoking
a cigarette, with an untasted salmi of something on his
plate and a half-empty bottle of Sauterne before him;
and he was quite silent. I said that the preparations
for the Jubilee made London impossible. (I rather
liked them, really.) I professed a wish to go right
away till the whole thing was over. In vain did I
attune myself to his gloom. He seemed not to hear me
nor even to see me. I felt that his behaviour made me
ridiculous in the eyes of the other man. The gangway
between the two rows of tables at the Vingtième was
hardly more than two feet wide (Rose and Berthe, in
their ministrations, had always to edge past each
other, quarrelling in whispers as they did so), and
any one at the table abreast of yours was practically
at yours. I thought our neighbour was amused at my
failure to interest Soames, and so, as I could not
explain to him that my insistence was merely charit-
able, I became silent. Without turning my head, I
had him well within my range of vision. I hoped I
looked less vulgar than he in contrast with Soames.
I was sure he was not an Englishman, but what *was*
his nationality? Though his jet-black hair was *en
brosse*, I did not think he was French. To Berthe,
who waited on him, he spoke French fluently, but
with a hardly native idiom and accent. I gathered

that this was his first visit to the Vingtième; but
Berthe was off-hand in her manner to him: he had
not made a good impression. His eyes were handsome, but—like the Vingtième's tables—too narrow
and set too close together. His nose was predatory,
and the points of his moustache, waxed up beyond
his nostrils, gave a fixity to his smile. Decidedly, he
was sinister. And my sense of discomfort in his presence was intensified by the scarlet waistcoat which
tightly, and so unseasonably in June, sheathed his
ample chest. This waistcoat wasn't wrong merely
because of the heat, either. It was somehow all wrong
in itself. It wouldn't have done on Christmas morning. It would have struck a jarring note at the first
night of 'Hernani.' I was trying to account for its
wrongness when Soames suddenly and strangely
broke silence. 'A hundred years hence!' he murmured, as in a trance.

'We shall not be here!' I briskly but fatuously
added.

'We shall not be here. No,' he droned, 'but the
Museum will still be just where it is. And the reading-
room, just where it is. And people will be able to go
and read there.' He inhaled sharply, and a spasm as
of actual pain contorted his features.

I wondered what train of thought poor Soames
had been following. He did not enlighten me when
he said, after a long pause, 'You think I haven't
minded.'

'Minded what, Soames?'

'Neglect. Failure.'

'*Failure?*' I said heartily. 'Failure?' I repeated

vaguely. 'Neglect—yes, perhaps; but that's quite another matter. Of course you haven't been—appreciated. But what then? Any artist who—who gives—' What I wanted to say was, 'Any artist who gives truly new and great things to the world has always to wait long for recognition'; but the flattery would not out: in the face of his misery, a misery so genuine and so unmasked, my lips would not say the words.

And then—he said them for me. I flushed. 'That's what you were going to say, isn't it?' he asked.

'How did you know?'

'It's what you said to me three years ago, when "Fungoids" was published.' I flushed the more. I need not have done so at all, for 'It's the only important thing I ever heard you say,' he continued. 'And I've never forgotten it. It's a true thing. It's a horrible truth. But—d'you remember what I answered? I said "I don't care a sou for recognition." And you believed me. You've gone on believing I'm above that sort of thing. You're shallow. What should *you* know of the feelings of a man like me? You imagine that a great artist's faith in himself and in the verdict of posterity is enough to keep him happy. . . . You've never guessed at the bitterness and loneliness, the'—his voice broke; but presently he resumed, speaking with a force that I had never known in him. 'Posterity! What use is it to *me*? A dead man doesn't know that people are visiting his grave—visiting his birthplace—putting up tablets to him—unveiling statues of him. A dead man can't read the books that are written about him.

A hundred years hence! Think of it! If I could come back to life *then*—just for a few hours—and go to the reading-room, and *read*! Or better still: if I could be projected, now, at this moment, into that future, into that reading-room, just for this one afternoon! I'd sell myself body and soul to the devil, for that! Think of the pages and pages in the catalogue: "SOAMES, ENOCH" endlessly—endless editions, commentaries, prolegomena, biographies'—but here he was interrupted by a sudden loud creak of the chair at the next table. Our neighbour had half risen from his place. He was leaning towards us, apologetically intrusive.

'Excuse—permit me,' he said softly. 'I have been unable not to hear. Might I take a liberty? In this little restaurant-sans-façon'—he spread wide his hands—'might I, as the phrase is, "cut in"?'

I could but signify our acquiescence. Berthe had appeared at the kitchen door, thinking the stranger wanted his bill. He waved her away with his cigar, and in another moment had seated himself beside me, commanding a full view of Soames.

'Though not an Englishman,' he explained, 'I know my London well, Mr. Soames. Your name and fame—Mr. Beerbohm's too—very known to me. Your point is: who am *I*?' He glanced quickly over his shoulder, and in a lowered voice said 'I am the Devil.'

I couldn't help it: I laughed. I tried not to, I knew there was nothing to laugh at, my rudeness shamed me, but—I laughed with increasing volume. The Devil's quiet dignity, the surprise and disgust of his raised eyebrows, did but the more dissolve me. I rocked to and fro, I lay back aching. I behaved deplorably.

'I am a gentleman, and,' he said with intense emphasis, 'I thought I was in the company of *gentlemen.*'

'Don't!' I gasped faintly. 'Oh, don't!'

'Curious, *nicht wahr?*' I heard him say to Soames. 'There is a type of person to whom the very mention of my name is—oh-so-awfully-funny! In your theatres the dullest comédien needs only to say "The Devil!" and right away they give him "the loud laugh that speaks the vacant mind." Is it not so?'

I had now just breath enough to offer my apologies. He accepted them, but coldly, and readdressed himself to Soames.

'I am a man of business,' he said, 'and always I would put things through "right now," as they say in the States. You are a poet. *Les affaires*—you detest them. So be it. But with me you will deal, eh? What you have said just now gives me furiously to hope.'

Soames had not moved, except to light a fresh cigarette. He sat crouched forward, with his elbows squared on the table, and his head just above the level of his hands, staring up at the Devil. 'Go on,' he nodded. I had no remnant of laughter in me now.

'It will be the more pleasant, our little deal,' the Devil went on, 'because you are—I mistake not?—a Diabolist.'

'A Catholic Diabolist,' said Soames.

The Devil accepted the reservation genially. 'You

wish,' he resumed, 'to visit now—this afternoon as-ever-is—the reading-room of the British Museum, yes? but of a hundred years hence, yes? *Parfaite-ment*. Time—an illusion. Past and future—they are as ever-present as the present, or at any rate only what you call "just-round-the-corner." I switch you on to any date. I project you—pouf! You wish to be in the reading-room just as it will be on the after-noon of June 3rd, 1997? You wish to find yourself standing in that room, just past the swing-doors, this very minute, yes? and to stay there till closing time? Am I right?'

Soames nodded.

The Devil looked at his watch. 'Ten past two,' he said. 'Closing time in summer same then as now: seven o'clock. That will give you almost five hours. At seven o'clock—pouf!—you find yourself again here, sitting at this table. I am dining to-night *dans le monde—dans le higlif*. That concludes my present visit to your great city. I come and fetch you here, Mr. Soames, on my way home.'

'Home?' I echoed.

'Be it never so humble!' said the Devil lightly.

'All right,' said Soames.

'Soames!' I entreated. But my friend moved not a muscle.

The Devil had made as though to stretch forth his hand across the table and touch Soames' forearm; but he paused in his gesture.

'A hundred years hence, as now,' he smiled, 'no smoking allowed in the reading-room. You would better therefore——'

Soames removed the cigarette from his mouth and dropped it into his glass of Sauterne.

'Soames!' again I cried. 'Can't you'—but the Devil had now stretched forth his hand across the table. He brought it slowly down on—the table-cloth. Soames' chair was empty. His cigarette floated sodden in his wine-glass. There was no other trace of him.

For a few moments the Devil let his hand rest where it lay, gazing at me out of the corners of his eyes, vulgarly triumphant.

A shudder shook me. With an effort I controlled myself and rose from my chair. 'Very clever,' I said condescendingly. 'But—"The Time Machine" is a delightful book, don't you think? So entirely original!'

'You are pleased to sneer,' said the Devil, who had also risen, 'but it is one thing to write about a not possible machine; it is a quite other thing to be a Supernatural Power.' All the same, I had scored.

Berthe had come forth at the sound of our rising. I explained to her that Mr. Soames had been called away, and that both he and I would be dining here. It was not until I was out in the open air that I began to feel giddy. I have but the haziest recollection of what I did, where I wandered, in the glaring sunshine of that endless afternoon. I remember the sound of carpenters' hammers all along Piccadilly, and the bare chaotic look of the half-erected 'stands.' Was it in the Green Park, or in Kensington Gardens, or *where* was it that I sat on a chair beneath a tree, trying to read an evening paper? There was a phrase in the leading article that went on repeating itself in

my fagged mind—'Little is hidden from this august
Lady full of the garnered wisdom of sixty years of
Sovereignty.' I remember wildly conceiving a letter
(to reach Windsor by express messenger told to await
answer):

'MADAM,—Well knowing that your Majesty is full
of the garnered wisdom of sixty years of Sovereignty,
I venture to ask your advice in the following delicate
matter. Mr. Enoch Soames, whose poems you may
or may not know,' . . .

Was there *no* way of helping him—saving him? A
bargain was a bargain, and I was the last man to aid
or abet any one in wriggling out of a reasonable
obligation. I wouldn't have lifted a little finger to save
Faust. But poor Soames!—doomed to pay without
respite an eternal price for nothing but a fruitless
search and a bitter disillusioning. . . .

Odd and uncanny it seemed to me that he, Soames,
in the flesh, in the waterproof cape, was at this
moment living in the last decade of the next century,
poring over books not yet written, and seeing and
seen by men not yet born. Uncannier and odder still,
that to-night and evermore he would be in Hell.
Assuredly, truth was stranger than fiction.

Endless that afternoon was. Almost I wished I had
gone with Soames—not indeed to stay in the reading-
room, but to sally forth for a brisk sight-seeing walk
around a new London. I wandered restlessly out of
the Park I had sat in. Vainly I tried to imagine myself an ardent tourist from the eighteenth century.
Intolerable was the strain of the slow-passing and

empty minutes. Long before seven o'clock I was back at the Vingtième.

I sat there just where I had sat for luncheon. Air came in listlessly through the open door behind me. Now and again Rose or Berthe appeared for a moment. I had told them I would not order any dinner till Mr. Soames came. A hurdy-gurdy began to play, abruptly drowning the noise of a quarrel between some Frenchmen further up the street. Whenever the tune was changed I heard the quarrel still raging. I had bought another evening paper on my way. I unfolded it. My eyes gazed ever away from it to the clock over the kitchen door. . . .

Five minutes, now, to the hour! I remembered that clocks in restaurants are kept five minutes fast. I concentrated my eyes on the paper. I vowed I would not look away from it again. I held it upright, at its full width, close to my face, so that I had no view of anything but it. . . . Rather a tremulous sheet? Only because of the draught, I told myself.

My arms gradually became stiff; they ached; but I could not drop them—now. I had a suspicion, I had a certainty. Well, what then? . . . What else had I come for? Yet I held tight that barrier of newspaper. Only the sound of Berthe's brisk footstep from the kitchen enabled me, forced me, to drop it, and to utter:

'What shall we have to eat, Soames?'

'*Il est souffrant, ce pauvre Monsieur Soames?*' asked Berthe.

'He's only—tired.' I asked her to get some wine —Burgundy—and whatever food might be ready.

Soames sat crouched forward against the table, exactly as when last I had seen him. It was as though he had never moved—he who had moved so unimaginably far. Once or twice in the afternoon it had for an instant occurred to me that perhaps his journey was not to be fruitless—that perhaps we had all been wrong in our estimate of the works of Enoch Soames. That we had been horribly right was horribly clear from the look of him. But 'Don't be discouraged,' I falteringly said. 'Perhaps it's only that you—didn't leave enough time. Two, three centuries hence, perhaps——'

'Yes,' his voice came. 'I've thought of that.'

'And now—now for the more immediate future! Where are you going to hide? How would it be if you caught the Paris express from Charing Cross? Almost an hour to spare. Don't go on to Paris. Stop at Calais. Live in Calais. He'd never think of looking for you in Calais.'

'It's like my luck,' he said, 'to spend my last hours on earth with an ass.' But I was not offended. 'And a treacherous ass,' he strangely added, tossing across to me a crumpled bit of paper which he had been holding in his hand. I glanced at the writing on it— some sort of gibberish, apparently. I laid it impatiently aside.

'Come, Soames! pull yourself together! This isn't a mere matter of life and death. It's a question of eternal torment, mind you! You don't mean to say you're going to wait limply here till the Devil comes to fetch you?'

'I can't do anything else. I've no choice.'

'Come! This is "trusting and encouraging" with a vengeance! This is Diabolism run mad!' I filled his glass with wine. 'Surely, now that you've *seen* the brute——'

'It's no good abusing him.'

'You must admit there's nothing Miltonic about him, Soames.'

'I don't say he's not rather different from what I expected.'

'He's a vulgarian, he's a swell-mobsman, he's the sort of man who hangs about the corridors of trains going to the Riviera and steals ladies' jewel-cases. Imagine eternal torment presided over by *him*!'

'You don't suppose I look forward to it, do you?'

'Then why not slip quietly out of the way?'

Again and again I filled his glass, and always, mechanically, he emptied it; but the wine kindled no spark of enterprise in him. He did not eat, and I myself ate hardly at all. I did not in my heart believe that any dash for freedom could save him. The chase would be swift, the capture certain. But better anything than this passive, meek, miserable waiting. I told Soames that for the honour of the human race he ought to make some show of resistance. He asked what the human race had ever done for him. 'Besides,' he said, 'can't you understand that I'm in his power? You saw him touch me, didn't you? There's an end of it. I've no will. I'm sealed.'

I made a gesture of despair. He went on repeating the word 'sealed.' I began to realise that the wine had clouded his brain. No wonder! Foodless he had gone into futurity, foodless he still was. I urged him to eat at any rate some bread. It was maddening to think that he, who had so much to tell, might tell nothing. 'How was it all,' I asked, 'yonder? Come! Tell me your adventures.'

'They'd make first-rate "copy," wouldn't they?'

'I'm awfully sorry for you, Soames, and I make all possible allowances; but what earthly right have you to insinuate that I should make "copy," as you call it, out of you?'

The poor fellow pressed his hands to his forehead. 'I don't know,' he said. 'I had some reason, I'm sure. . . . I'll try to remember.'

'That's right. Try to remember everything. Eat a little more bread. What did the reading-room look like?'

'Much as usual,' he at length muttered.

'Many people there?'

'Usual sort of number.'

'What did they look like?'

Soames tried to visualise them. 'They all,' he presently remembered, 'looked very like one another.'

My mind took a fearsome leap. 'All dressed in Jaeger?'

'Yes. I think so. Greyish-yellowish stuff.'

'A sort of uniform?' He nodded. 'With a number on it, perhaps?—a number on a large disc of metal sewn on to the left sleeve? DKF 78,910—that sort of thing?' It was even so. 'And all of them—men and women alike—looking very well-cared-for? very Utopian? and smelling rather strongly of carbolic? and all of them quite hairless?' I was right every time.

Soames was only not sure whether the men and women were hairless or shorn. 'I hadn't time to look at them very closely,' he explained.

'No, of course not. But—'

'They stared at *me*, I can tell you. I attracted a great deal of attention.' At last he had done that! 'I think I rather scared them. They moved away whenever I came near. They followed me about at a distance, wherever I went. The men at the round desk in the middle seemed to have a sort of panic whenever I went to make inquiries.'

'What did you do when you arrived?'

Well, he had gone straight to the catalogue, of course—to the S volumes, and had stood long before SN–SOF, unable to take this volume out of the shelf, because his heart was beating so. . . . At first, he said, he wasn't disappointed—he only thought there was some new arrangement. He went to the middle desk and asked where the catalogue of *twentieth*-century books was kept. He gathered that there was still only one catalogue. Again he looked up his name, stared at the three little pasted slips he had known so well. Then he went and sat down for a long time. . . .

'And then,' he droned, 'I looked up the "Dictionary of National Biography" and some encyclopædias. . . . I went back to the middle desk and asked what was the best modern book on late nineteenth-century literature. They told me Mr. T. K. Nupton's book was considered the best. I looked it up in the catalogue and filled in a form for it. It was brought to me. My name wasn't in the index, but— Yes!' he said with a sudden change of tone. 'That's what I'd forgotten. Where's that bit of paper? Give it me back.'

I, too, had forgotten that cryptic screed. I found it fallen on the floor, and handed it to him.

He smoothed it out, nodding and smiling at me disagreeably. 'I found myself glancing through Nupton's book,' he resumed. 'Not very easy reading. Some sort of phonetic spelling. . . . All the modern books I saw were phonetic.'

'Then I don't want to hear any more, Soames, please.'

'The proper names seemed all to be spelt in the old way. But for that, I mightn't have noticed my own name.'

'Your own name? Really? Soames, I'm *very* glad.'

'And yours.'

'No!'

'I thought I should find you waiting here to-night. So I took the trouble to copy out the passage. Read it.'

I snatched the paper. Soames' handwriting was characteristically dim. It, and the noisome spelling, and my excitement, made me all the slower to grasp what T. K. Nupton was driving at.

The document lies before me at this moment. Strange that the words I here copy out for you were copied out for me by poor Soames just seventy-eight years hence. . . .

From p. 234 of 'Inglish Littracher 1890–1900,' bi T. K. Nupton, published bi th Stait, 1992:

'Fr. egzarmpl, a riter ov th time, naimd Max
Beerbohm, hoo woz stil alive in th twentieth senchri,
rote a stauri in wich e pautraid an immajnari karrakter
kauld "Enoch Soames"—a thurd-rait poit hoo
beleevz imself a grate jeneus an maix a bargin with
th Devvl in auder ter no wot posterriti thinx ov im!
It iz a sumwot labud sattire but not without vallu az
showing hou seriusli the yung men ov th aiteen-
ninetiz took themselvz. Nou that the littreri profeshn
haz bin auganized az a department of publik servis,
our riters hav found their levvl an hav lernt ter doo
their duti without thort ov th morro. "Th laibrer iz
werthi ov hiz hire," an that iz aul. Thank hevvn we
hav no Enoch Soameses amung us to-dai!'

I found that by murmuring the words aloud (a
device which I commend to my reader) I was able
to master them, little by little. The clearer they became, the greater was my bewilderment, my distress
and horror. The whole thing was a nightmare. Afar,
the great grisly background of what was in store
for the poor dear art of letters; here, at the table,
fixing on me a gaze that made me hot all over, the
poor fellow whom—whom evidently . . . but no:
whatever down-grade my character might take in
coming years, I should never be such a brute as
to——

Again I examined the screed. 'Immajnari'—but
here Soames was, no more imaginary, alas! than I.
And 'labud'—what on earth was that? (To this day,
I have never made out that word.) 'It's all very—
baffling,' I at length stammered.

Soames said nothing, but cruelly did not cease to look at me.

'Are you sure,' I temporised, 'quite sure you copied the thing out correctly?'

'Quite.'

'Well, then it's this wretched Nupton who must have made—must be going to make—some idiotic mistake. . . . Look here, Soames! you know me better than to suppose that I . . . After all, the name "Max Beerbohm" is not at all an uncommon one, and there must be several Enoch Soameses running around— or rather, "Enoch Soames" is a name that might occur to any one writing a story. And I don't write stories: I'm an essayist, an observer, a recorder. . . . I admit that it's an extraordinary coincidence. But you must see——'

'I see the whole thing,' said Soames quietly. And he added, with a touch of his old manner, but with more dignity than I had ever known in him, '*Parlons d'autre chose.*'

I accepted that suggestion very promptly. I returned straight to the more immediate future. I spent most of the long evening in renewed appeals to Soames to slip away and seek refuge somewhere. I remember saying at last that if indeed I was destined to write about him, the supposed 'stauri' had better have at least a happy ending. Soames repeated those last three words in a tone of intense scorn. 'In Life and in Art,' he said, 'all that matters is an *inevitable* ending.'

'But,' I urged, more hopefully than I felt, 'an ending that can be avoided *isn't* inevitable.'

'You aren't an artist,' he rasped. 'And you're so hopelessly not an artist that, so far from being able to imagine a thing and make it seem true, you're going to make even a true thing seem as if you'd made it up. You're a miserable bungler. And it's like my luck.'

I protested that the miserable bungler was not I—was not going to be I—but T. K. Nupton; and we had a rather heated argument, in the thick of which it suddenly seemed to me that Soames saw he was in the wrong: he had quite physically cowered. But I wondered why—and now I guessed with a cold throb just why—he stared so, past me. The bringer of that 'inevitable ending' filled the door-way.

I managed to turn in my chair and to say, not without a semblance of lightness, 'Aha, come in!' Dread was indeed rather blunted in me by his looking so absurdly like a villain in a melodrama. The sheen of his tilted hat and of his shirtfront, the repeated twists he was giving to his moustache, and most of all the magnificence of his sneer, gave token that he was there only to be foiled.

He was at our table in a stride. 'I am sorry,' he sneered witheringly, 'to break up your pleasant party, but—'

'You don't: you complete it,' I assured him. 'Mr. Soames and I want to have a little talk with you. Won't you sit? Mr. Soames got nothing—frankly nothing—by his journey this afternoon. We don't wish to say that the whole thing was a swindle—a common swindle. On the contrary, we believe you meant well. But of course the bargain, such as it was, is off.'

The Devil gave no verbal answer. He merely looked at Soames and pointed with rigid forefinger to the door. Soames was wretchedly rising from his chair when, with a desperate quick gesture, I swept together two dinner-knives that were on the table, and laid their blades across each other. The Devil stepped sharp back against the table behind him, averting his face and shuddering.

'You are not superstitious!' he hissed.

'Not at all,' I smiled.

'Soames!' he said as to an underling, but without turning his face, 'put those knives straight!'

With an inhibitive gesture to my friend, 'Mr. Soames,' I said emphatically to the Devil, 'is a *Catholic* Diabolist'; but my poor friend did the Devil's bidding, not mine; and now, with his master's eyes again fixed on him, he arose, he shuffled past me. I tried to speak. It was he that spoke. 'Try,' was the prayer he threw back at me as the Devil pushed him roughly out through the door, '*try* to make them know that I did exist!'

In another instant I too was through that door. I stood staring all ways—up the street, across it, down it. There was moonlight and lamplight, but there was not Soames nor that other.

Dazed, I stood there. Dazed, I turned back, at length, into the little room; and I suppose I paid Berthe or Rose for my dinner and luncheon, and for Soames': I hope so, for I never went to the Vingtième again. Ever since that night I have avoided Greek

Street altogether. And for years I did not set foot even in Soho Square, because on that same night it was there that I paced and loitered, long and long, with some such dull sense of hope as a man has in not straying far from the place where he has lost something. . . . 'Round and round the shutter'd Square'—that line came back to me on my lonely beat, and with it the whole stanza, ringing in my brain and bearing in on me how tragically different from the happy scene imagined by him was the poet's actual experience of that prince in whom of all princes we should put not our trust.

But—strange how the mind of an essayist, be it never so stricken, roves and ranges!—I remember pausing before a wide doorstep and wondering if perchance it was on this very one that the young De Quincey lay ill and faint while poor Ann flew as fast as her feet would carry her to Oxford Street, the 'stony-hearted stepmother' of them both, and came back bearing that 'glass of port wine and spices' but for which he might, so he thought, actually have died. Was this the very doorstep that the old De Quincey used to revisit in homage? I pondered Ann's fate, the cause of her sudden vanishing from the ken of her boy-friend; and presently I blamed myself for letting the past over-ride the present. Poor vanished Soames!

And for myself, too, I began to be troubled. What had I better do? Would there be a hue and cry— Mysterious Disappearance of an Author, and all that? He had last been seen lunching and dining in my company. Hadn't I better get a hansom and drive straight to Scotland Yard? . . . They would think I was a lunatic. After all, I reassured myself, London was a very large place, and one very dim figure might easily drop out of it unobserved—now especially, in the blinding glare of the near Jubilee. Better say nothing at all, I thought.

And I was right. Soames' disappearance made no stir at all. He was utterly forgotten before any one, so far as I am aware, noticed that he was no longer hanging around. Now and again some poet or prosaist may have said to another, 'What has become of that man Soames?' but I never heard any such question asked. The solicitor through whom he was paid his annuity may be presumed to have made inquiries, but no echo of these resounded. There was something rather ghastly to me in the general unconsciousness that Soames had existed, and more than once I caught myself wondering whether Nupton, that babe unborn, were going to be right in thinking him a figment of my brain.

In that extract from Nupton's repulsive book there is one point which perhaps puzzles you. How is it that the author, though I have here mentioned him by name and have quoted the exact words he is going to write, is not going to grasp the obvious corollary that I have invented nothing? The answer can but be this: Nupton will not have read the later passages of this memoir. Such lack of thoroughness is a serious fault in any one who undertakes to do scholar's work. And I hope these words will meet the eye of some contemporary rival to Nupton and be the undoing of Nupton.

I like to think that some time between 1992 and 1997 somebody will have looked up this memoir, and will have forced on the world his inevitable and startling conclusions. And I have reasons for believing that this will be so. You realise that the reading-room into which Soames was projected by the Devil was in all respects precisely as it will be on the afternoon of June 3rd, 1997. You realise, therefore, that on that afternoon, when it comes round, there the self-same crowd will be, and there Soames too will be, punctually, he and they doing precisely what they did before. Recall now Soames' account of the sensation he made. You may say that the mere difference of his costume was enough to make him sensational in that uniformed crowd. You wouldn't say so if you had ever seen him. I assure you that in no period could Soames be anything but dim. The fact that people are going to stare at him, and follow him around, and seem afraid of him, can be explained only on the hypothesis that they will somehow have been prepared for his ghostly visitation. They will have been awfully waiting to see whether he really would come. And when he does come the effect will of course be—awful.

An authentic, guaranteed, proven ghost, but—only a ghost, alas! Only that. In his first visit, Soames was a creature of flesh and blood, whereas the creatures into whose midst he was projected were but ghosts, I take it—solid, palpable, vocal, but unconscious and automatic ghosts, in a building that was itself an illusion. Next time, that building and those creatures will be real. It is of Soames that there will be but the semblance. I wish I could think him destined to revisit the world actually, physically, consciously. I wish he had this one brief escape, this one small treat, to look forward to. I never forget him for long. He is where he is, and forever. The more rigid moralists among you may say he has only himself to blame. For my part, I think he has been very hardly used. It is well that vanity should be chastened; and Enoch Soames' vanity was, I admit, above the average, and called for special treatment. But there was no need for vindictiveness. You say he contracted to pay the price he is paying; yes; but I maintain that he was induced to do so by fraud. Well-informed in all things, the Devil must have known that my friend would gain nothing by his visit to futurity. The whole thing was a very shabby trick. The more I think of it, the more detestable the Devil seems to me.

Of him I have caught sight several times, here and there, since that day at the Vingtième. Only once, however, have I seen him at close quarters. This was in Paris. I was walking, one afternoon, along the Rue d'Antin, when I saw him advancing from the opposite direction—over-dressed as ever, and swinging an ebony cane, and altogether behaving as though the whole pavement belonged to him. At thought of Enoch Soames and the myriads of other sufferers eternally in this brute's dominion, a great cold wrath filled me, and I drew myself up to my full height. But—well, one is so used to nodding and smiling in the street to anybody whom one knows, that the action becomes almost independent of oneself: to prevent it requires a very sharp effort and great presence of mind. I was miserably aware, as I passed the Devil, that I nodded and smiled to him. And my shame was the deeper and hotter because he, if you please, stared straight at me with the utmost haughtiness.

To be cut—deliberately cut—by *him*! I was, I still am, furious at having had that happen to me.

HILARY MALTBY AND
STEPHEN BRAXTON

HILARY MALTBY AND
STEPHEN BRAXTON

1917

PEOPLE still go on comparing Thackeray and
Dickens, quite cheerfully. But the fashion of comparing Maltby and Braxton went out so long ago as
1795. No, I am wrong. But anything that happened
in the bland old days before the War does seem to be
a hundred more years ago than actually it is. The
year I mean is the one in whose spring-time we all
went bicycling (O thrill!) in Battersea Park, and
ladies wore sleeves that billowed enormously out
from their shoulders, and Lord Rosebery was Prime
Minister.

In that Park, in that spring-time, in that sea of
sleeves, there was almost as much talk about the
respective merits of Braxton and Maltby as there was
about those of Rudge and Humber. For the benefit
of my younger readers, and perhaps, so feeble is
human memory, for the benefit of their elders too,
let me state that Rudge and Humber were rival
makers of bicycles, that Hilary Maltby was the author
of 'Ariel in Mayfair,' and Stephen Braxton of 'A
Faun on the Cotswolds.'

'Which do you think is *really* the best—"Ariel"
or "A Faun"?' Ladies were always asking one that
question. 'Oh, well, you know, the two are so different. It's really very hard to compare them.' One

was always giving that answer. One was not very
brilliant perhaps.

The vogue of the two novels lasted throughout
the summer. As both were 'firstlings,' and Great
Britain had therefore nothing else of Braxton's or
Maltby's to fall back on, the horizon was much
scanned for what Maltby, and what Braxton, would
give us next. In the autumn Braxton gave us his
secondling. It was an instantaneous failure. No more
was Braxton compared with Maltby. In the spring of
'96 came Maltby's secondling. Its failure was instantaneous. Maltby might once more have been compared with Braxton. But Braxton was now forgotten.
So was Maltby.

This was not kind. This was not just. Maltby's
first novel, and Braxton's, had brought delight into
many thousands of homes. People should have
paused to say of Braxton 'Perhaps his third novel
will be better than his second,' and to say as much
for Maltby. I blame people for having given no sign
of wanting a third from either; and I blame them
with the more zest because neither 'A Faun on the
Cotswolds' nor 'Ariel in Mayfair' was a merely
popular book: each, I maintain, was a good book.
I don't go so far as to say that the one had 'more of
natural magic, more of British woodland glamour,
more of the sheer joy of life in it than anything since
"As You Like It",' though Higsby went so far as
this in the *Daily Chronicle*; nor can I allow the claim
made for the other by Grigsby in the *Globe* that 'for
pungency of satire there has been nothing like it since
Swift laid down his pen, and for sheer sweetness and

tenderness of feeling—*ex forti dulcedo*—nothing to be mentioned in the same breath with it since the lute fell from the tired hand of Theocritus.' These were foolish exaggerations. But one must not condemn a thing because it has been over-praised. Maltby's 'Ariel' was a delicate, brilliant work; and Braxton's 'Faun,' crude though it was in many ways, had yet a genuine power and beauty. This is not a mere impression remembered from early youth. It is the reasoned and seasoned judgment of middle age. Both books have been out of print for many years; but I secured a second-hand copy of each not long ago, and found them well worth reading again.

From the time of Nathaniel Hawthorne to the outbreak of the War, current literature did not suffer from any lack of fauns. But when Braxton's first book appeared fauns had still an air of novelty about them. We had not yet tired of them and their hoofs and their slanting eyes and their way of coming suddenly out of woods to wean quiet English villages from respectability. We did tire later. But Braxton's faun, even now, seems to me an admirable specimen of his class—wild and weird, earthly, goat-like, almost convincing. And I find myself convinced altogether by Braxton's rustics. I admit that I do not know much about rustics, except from novels. But I plead that the little I do know about them by personal observation does not confirm much of what the many novelists have taught me. I plead also that Braxton may well have been right about the rustics of Gloucestershire because he was (as so many interviewers recorded of him in his brief heyday) the son of a yeoman farmer at Far Oakridge, and his boyhood had been divided between that village and the Grammar School at Stroud. Not long ago I happened to be staying in the neighbourhood, and came across several villagers who might, I assure you, have stepped straight out of Braxton's pages. For that matter, Braxton himself, whom I met often in the spring of '95, might have stepped straight out of his own pages.

I am guilty of having wished he would step straight back into them. He was a very surly fellow, very rugged and gruff. He was the antithesis of pleasant little Maltby. I used to think that perhaps he would have been less unamiable if success had come to him earlier. He was thirty years old when his book was published, and had had a very hard time since coming to London at the age of sixteen. Little Maltby was a year older, and so had waited a year longer; but then, he had waited under a comfortable roof at Twickenham, emerging into the metropolis for no grimmer purpose than to sit and watch the fashionable riders and walkers in Rotten Row, and then going home to write a little, or to play lawn-tennis with the young ladies of Twickenham. He had been the only child of his parents (neither of whom, alas, survived to take pleasure in their darling's sudden fame). He had now migrated from Twickenham and taken rooms in Ryder Street. Had he ever shared with Braxton the bread of adversity—but no, I think he would in any case have been pleasant. And conversely I cannot imagine that Braxton would in any case have been so.

No one seeing the two rivals together, no one meeting them at Mr. Hookworth's famous luncheon parties in the Authors' Club, or at Mrs. Foster-Dugdale's not less famous garden parties in Greville Place, would have supposed off-hand that the pair had a single point in common. Dapper little Maltby—blond, bland, diminutive Maltby, with his monocle and his gardenia; big black Braxton, with his lanky hair and his square blue jaw and his square sallow forehead. Canary and crow. Maltby had a perpetual chirrup of amusing small-talk. Braxton was usually silent, but very well worth listening to whenever he did croak. He had distinction, I admit it; the distinction of one who steadfastly refuses to adapt himself to surroundings. He stood out. He awed Mr. Hookworth. Ladies were always asking one another, rather intently, what they thought of him. One could imagine that Mr. Foster-Dugdale, had he come home from the City to attend the garden parties, might have regarded him as one from whom Mrs. Foster-Dugdale should be shielded. But the casual observer of Braxton and Maltby at Mrs. Foster-Dugdale's or elsewhere was wrong in supposing that the two were totally unlike. He overlooked one simple and obvious point. This was that he had met them both at Mrs. Foster-Dugdale's or elsewhere. Wherever they were invited, there certainly, there punctually, they would be. They were both of them gluttons for the fruits and signs of their success.

Interviewers and photographers had as little reason as had hostesses to complain of two men so earnestly and assiduously 'on the make' as Maltby and Braxton.

Maltby, for all his sparkle, was earnest; Braxton, for
all his arrogance, assiduous.

'A Faun on the Cotswolds' had no more eager
eulogist then the author of 'Ariel in Mayfair.' When
any one praised his work, Maltby would lightly dis-
parage it in comparison with Braxton's—'Ah, if I
could write like *that*!' Maltby won golden opinions
in this way. Braxton, on the other hand, would let
slip no opportunity for sneering at Maltby's work—
'gimcrack,' as he called it. This was not good for
Maltby. Different men, different methods.

'The Rape of the Lock' was 'gimcrack,' if you care
to call it so; but it was a delicate, brilliant work; and
so, I repeat, was Maltby's 'Ariel.' Absurd to compare
Maltby with Pope? I am not so sure. I have read
'Ariel,' but have never read 'The Rape of the Lock.'
Braxton's opprobrious term for 'Ariel' may not, however, have been due to jealousy alone. Braxton had
imagination, and his rival did not soar above fancy.
But the point is that Maltby's fancifulness went far
and well. In telling how Ariel re-embodied himself
from thin air, leased a small house in Chesterfield
Street, was presented at a Levée, played the part of
good fairy in a matter of true love not running smooth,
and worked meanwhile all manner of amusing
changes among the aristocracy before he vanished
again, Maltby showed a very pretty range of in-
genuity. In one respect, his work was a more sur-
prising achievement than Braxton's. For, whereas
Braxton had been born and bred among his rustics,
Maltby knew his aristocrats only through Thackeray,
through the photographs and paragraphs in the news-

papers, and through those passionate excursions of his to Rotten Row. Yet I found his aristocrats as convincing as Braxton's rustics. It is true that I may have been convinced wrongly. That is a point which I could settle only by experience. I shift my ground, claiming for Maltby's aristocrats just this: that they pleased me very much.

Aristocrats, when they are presented solely through a novelist's sense of beauty, do not satisfy us. They may be as beautiful as all that, but, for fear of thinking ourselves snobbish, we won't believe it. We do believe it, however, and revel in it, when the novelist saves his face and ours by a pervading irony in the treatment of what he loves. The irony must, mark you, be pervading and obvious. Disraeli's great ladies and lords won't do, for his irony was but latent in his homage, and thus the reader feels himself called on to worship and in duty bound to scoff. All's well, though, when the homage is latent in the irony. Thackeray, inviting us to laugh and frown over the follies of Mayfair, enables us to reel with him in a secret orgy of veneration for those fools.

Maltby, too, in his measure, enabled us to reel thus. That is mainly why, before the end of April, his publisher was in a position to state that 'the Seventh Large Impression of "Ariel in Mayfair" is almost exhausted.' Let it be put to our credit, however, that at the same moment Braxton's publisher had 'the honour to inform the public that an Eighth Large Impression of "A Faun on the Cotswolds" is in instant preparation.'

Indeed, it seemed impossible for either author to

outvie the other in success and glory. Week in, week out, you saw cancelled either's every momentary advantage. A neck-and-neck race. As thus:—Maltby appears as a Celebrity At Home in the *World* (Tuesday). Ha! No, *Vanity Fair* (Wednesday) has a perfect presentment of Braxton by 'Spy.' Neck-and-neck! No, *Vanity Fair* says 'the subject of next week's cartoon will be Mr. Hilary Maltby.' Maltby wins! No, next week Braxton's in the *World*.

Throughout May I kept, as it were, my eyes glued to my field-glasses. On the first Monday in June I saw that which drew from me a hoarse ejaculation.

Let me explain that always on Monday mornings at this time of year, when I opened my daily paper, I looked with respectful interest to see what bevy of the great world had been entertained since Saturday at Keeb Hall. The list was always august and inspiring. Statecraft and Diplomacy were well threaded there with mere Lineage and mere Beauty, with Royalty sometimes, with mere Wealth never, with privileged Genius now and then. A noble composition always. It was said that the Duke of Hertfordshire cared for nothing but his collection of birds' eggs, and that the collections of guests at Keeb were formed entirely by his young Duchess. It was said that he had climbed trees in every corner of every continent. The Duchess' hobby was easier. She sat aloft and beckoned desirable specimens up.

The list published on that first Monday in June began ordinarily enough, began with the Austro-Hungarian Ambassador and the Portuguese Minister. Then came the Duke and Duchess of Mull, followed by four lesser Peers (two of them Proconsuls, however) with their Peeresses, three Peers without their Peeresses, four Peeresses without their Peers, and a dozen bearers of courtesy-titles with or without their wives or husbands. The rear was brought up by 'Mr. A. J. Balfour, Mr. Henry Chaplin, and Mr. Hilary Maltby.'

Youth tends to look at the darker side of things. I confess that my first thought was for Braxton.

I forgave and forgot his faults of manner. Youth is generous. It does not criticise a strong man stricken.

And anon, so habituated was I to the parity of those two strivers, I conceived that there might be some mistake. Daily newspapers are printed in a hurry. Might not 'Henry Chaplin' be a typographical error for 'Stephen Braxton'? I went out and bought another newspaper. But Mr. Chaplin's name was in that too.

'Patience!' I said to myself. 'Braxton crouches only to spring. He will be at Keeb Hall on Saturday next.'

My mind was free now to dwell with pleasure on Maltby's great achievement. I thought of writing to congratulate him, but feared this might be in bad taste. I did, however, write asking him to lunch with me. He did not answer my letter. I was, therefore, all the more sorry, next Monday, at not finding 'and Mr. Stephen Braxton' in Keeb's week-end catalogue.

A few days later I met Mr. Hookworth. He mentioned that Stephen Braxton had left town. 'He has taken,' said Hookworth, 'a delightful bungalow on the east coast. He has gone there to *work*.' He added that he had a great liking for Braxton—'a man utterly *unspoilt.*' I inferred that he, too, had written to Maltby and received no answer.

That butterfly did not, however, appear to be hovering from flower to flower in the parterres of rank and fashion. In the daily lists of guests at dinners, receptions, dances, balls, the name of Maltby figured never. Maltby had not caught on.

Presently I heard that he, too, had left town. I gathered that he had gone quite early in June—quite soon after Keeb. Nobody seemed to know where he was. My own theory was that he had taken a delightful bungalow on the west coast, to balance Braxton. Anyhow, the parity of the two strivers was now somewhat re-established.

In point of fact, the disparity had been less than I supposed. While Maltby was at Keeb, there Braxton was also—in a sense. . . . It was a strange story. I did not hear it at the time. Nobody did. I heard it seventeen years later. I heard it in Lucca.

Little Lucca I found so enchanting that, though I had only a day or two to spare, I stayed there a whole month. I formed the habit of walking, every morning, round that high-pitched path which girdles Lucca, that wide and tree-shaded path from which one looks down over the city wall at the fertile plains beneath Lucca. There were never many people there; but the few who did come came daily, so that I grew to like seeing them and took a mild personal interest in them.

One of them was an old lady in a wheeled chair.

She was not less than seventy years old, and might or might not have once been beautiful. Her chair was slowly propelled by an Italian woman. She herself was obviously Italian. Not so, however, the little gentleman who walked assiduously beside her. Him I guessed to be English. He was a very stout little gentleman, with gleaming spectacles and a full blond beard, and he seemed to radiate cheerfulness. I thought at first that he might be the old lady's resident physician; but no, there was something subtly un-professional about him: I became sure that his constancy was gratuitous, and his radiance real. And one day, I know not how, there dawned on me a suspicion that he was—who?—some one I had known—some writer—what's-his-name—something with an M—Maltby—Hilary Maltby of the long-ago!

At sight of him on the morrow this suspicion hardened almost to certainty. I wished I could meet him alone and ask him if I were not right, and what he had been doing all these years, and why he had left England. He was always with the old lady. It was only on my last day in Lucca that my chance came.

I had just lunched, and was seated on a comfortable bench outside my hotel, with a cup of coffee on the table before me, gazing across the faded old sunny piazza and wondering what to do with my last afternoon. It was then that I espied yonder the back of the putative Maltby. I hastened forth to him. He was buying some pink roses, a great bunch of them, from a market-woman under an umbrella. He looked very blank, he flushed greatly, when I ventured to accost him. He admitted that his name was Hilary Maltby.

I told him my own name, and by degrees he remembered me. He apologised for his confusion. He explained that he had not talked English, had not
talked to an Englishman, 'for—oh, hundreds of
years.' He said that he had, in the course of his long
residence in Lucca, seen two or three people whom
he had known in England, but that none of them had
recognised him. He accepted (but as though he were
embarking on the oddest adventure in the world) my
invitation that he should come and sit down and take
coffee with me. He laughed with pleasure and surprise at finding that he could still speak his native
tongue quite fluently and idiomatically. 'I know
absolutely nothing,' he said, 'about England nowadays—except from stray references to it in the
Corriere della Sera'; nor did he show the faintest
desire that I should enlighten him. 'England,' he
mused, '—how it all comes back to me!'

'But not you to it?'

'Ah, no indeed,' he said gravely, looking at the
roses which he had laid carefully on the marble table.
'I am the happiest of men.'

He sipped his coffee, and stared out across the
piazza, out beyond it into the past.

'I am the happiest of men,' he repeated. I plied
him with the spur of silence.

'And I owe it all to having once yielded to a bad
impulse. Absurd, the threads our destinies hang on!'

Again I plied him with that spur. As it seemed not
to prick him, I repeated the words he had last spoken.
'For instance?' I added.

'Take,' he said, 'a certain evening in the spring of

'95. Suppose the Duchess of Hertfordshire had had a bad cold that evening. If she had had that, or a headache, or if she had decided that it *wouldn't* be rather interesting to go on to that party—that Annual Soirée, I think it was—of the Inkwomen's Club; or again—to go a step further back—if she hadn't ever written that one little poem, and if it *hadn't* been printed in "The Gentlewoman," and if the Inkwomen's committee *hadn't* instantly and unanimously elected her an Honorary Vice-President because of that one little poem; or if—well, if a million-and-one utterly irrelevant things hadn't happened, don't-you-know, I shouldn't be here . . . I might be *there*,' he smiled, with a vague gesture indicating England.

'Suppose,' he went on, 'I hadn't been invited to that Annual Soirée; or suppose that other fellow,—'

'Braxton?' I suggested. I had remembered Braxton at the moment of recognising Maltby.

'Suppose *he* hadn't been asked. . . . But of course we both were. It happened that I was the first to be presented to the Duchess. . . . It was a great moment. I hoped I should keep my head. She wore a tiara. I had often seen women in tiaras, at the Opera. But I had never talked to a woman in a tiara. Tiaras were symbols to me. Eyes are just a human feature. I fixed mine on the Duchess's. I kept my head by not looking at hers. I behaved as one human being to another. She seemed very intelligent. We got on very well. Presently she asked whether I should think her *very* bold if she said how *perfectly* divine she thought my book. I said something about doing my best, and

asked with animation whether she had read "A Faun
on the Cotswolds." She had. She said it was *too*
wonderful, she said it was *too* great. If she hadn't
been a Duchess, I might have thought her slightly
hysterical. Her innate good-sense quickly reasserted
itself. She used her great power. With a wave of her
magic wand she turned into a fact the glittering possibility that had haunted me. She asked me down to
Keeb.

'She seemed very pleased that I would come. Was
I, by any chance, free on Saturday week? She hoped
there would be some amusing people to meet me.
Could I come by the 3.30? It was only an hour-and-
a-quarter from Victoria. On Saturday there were
always compartments reserved for people coming to
Keeb by the 3.30. She hoped I would bring my
bicycle with me. She hoped I wouldn't find it very
dull. She hoped I wouldn't forget to come. She said
how lovely it must be to spend one's life among
clever people. She supposed I knew everybody here
to-night. She asked me to tell her who everybody was.
She asked who was the tall, dark man, over there. I
told her it was Stephen Braxton. She said they had
promised to introduce her to him. She added that he
looked rather wonderful. "Oh, he is, very," I assured
her. She turned to me with a sudden appeal: "*Do*
you think, if I took my courage in both hands and
asked him, he'd care to come to Keeb?"

'I hesitated. It would be easy to say that Satan
answered *for* me; easy but untrue; it was I that
babbled: "Well—as a matter of fact—since you ask
me—if I were you—really I think you'd better not.

He's very odd in some ways. He has an extraordinary hatred of sleeping out of London. He has the real Gloucestershire *love* of London. At the same time, he's very shy; and if you asked him he wouldn't very well know how to refuse. I think it would be *kinder* not to ask him."

'At that moment, Mrs. Wilpham—the President— loomed up to us, bringing Braxton. He bore himself well. Rough dignity with a touch of mellowness. I daresay you never saw him smile. He smiled gravely down at the Duchess, while she talked in her pretty little quick humble way. He made a great impression.

'What I had done was not merely base: it was very dangerous. I was in terror that she might rally him on his devotion to London. I didn't dare to move away. I was immensely relieved when at length she said she must be going.

'Braxton seemed loth to relax his grip on her hand at parting. I feared she wouldn't escape without uttering that invitation. But all was well. . . . In saying good night to me, she added in a murmur, "Don't forget Keeb—Saturday week—the 3.30." Merely an exquisite murmur. But Braxton heard it. I knew, by the diabolical look he gave me, that Braxton had heard it. . . . If he hadn't, I shouldn't be here.

'Was I a prey to remorse? Well, in the days between that Soirée and that Saturday, remorse often claimed me, but rapture wouldn't give me up. Arcady, Olympus, the right people, at last! I hadn't realised how good my book was—not till it got me this guerdon; not till I got it this huge advertisement.

I foresaw how pleased my publisher would be. In some great houses, I had often heard, it was possible to stay without any one knowing you had been there. But the Duchess of Hertfordshire hid her light under no bushel. Exclusive she was, but not of publicity. Next to Windsor Castle, Keeb Hall was the most advertised house in all England.

'Meanwhile, I had plenty to do. I rather thought of engaging a valet, but decided that this wasn't necessary. On the other hand, I felt a need for three new summer suits, and a new evening suit, and some new white waistcoats. Also a smoking suit. And had any man ever stayed at Keeb without a dressing-case? Hitherto I had been content with a pair of wooden brushes, and so forth. I was afraid these would appal the footman who unpacked my things. I ordered, for his sake, a large dressing-case, with my initials engraved throughout it. It looked compromisingly new when it came to me from the shop. I had to kick it industriously, and throw it about and scratch it, so as to avert possible suspicion. The tailor did not send my things home till the Friday evening. I had to sit up late, wearing the new suits in rotation.

'Next day, at Victoria, I saw strolling on the platform many people, male and female, who looked as if they were going to Keeb—tall, cool, ornate people who hadn't packed their own things and had reached Victoria in broughams. I was ornate, but not tall nor cool. My porter was rather off-hand in his manner as he wheeled my things along to the 3.30. I asked severely if there were any compartments reserved for people going to stay with the Duke of Hertfordshire.

This worked an instant change in him. Having set me in one of those shrines, he seemed almost loth to accept a tip. A snob, I am afraid.

'A selection of the tall, the cool, the ornate, the intimately acquainted with one another, soon filled the compartment. There I was, and I think they felt they ought to try to bring me into the conversation. As they were all talking about a cotillion of the previous night, I shouldn't have been able to shine. I gazed out of the window, with middle-class aloofness. Presently the talk drifted on to the topic of bicycles. But by this time it was too late for me to come in.

'I gazed at the squalid outskirts of London as they flew by. I doubted, as I listened to my fellow-passengers, whether I should be able to shine at Keeb. I rather wished I were going to spend the week-end at one of those little houses with back-gardens beneath the railway-line. I was filled with fears.

'For shame! thought I. Was I nobody? Was the author of "Ariel in Mayfair" nobody?

'I reminded myself how glad Braxton would be if he knew of my faint-heartedness. I thought of Braxton sitting, at this moment, in his room in Clifford's Inn and glowering with envy of his hated rival in the 3.30. And after all, how enviable I was! My spirits rose. I would acquit myself well. . . .

'I much admired the scene at the little railway station where we alighted. It was like a *fête* by Lancret. I knew from the talk of my fellow-passengers that some people had been going down by an earlier train, and that others were coming by a later. But

the 3.30 had brought a full score of us. Us! That was
the final touch of beauty.

'Outside there were two broughams, a landau,
dog-carts, a phaeton, a wagonette, I know not what.
But almost everybody, it seemed, was going to
bicycle. Lady Rodfitten said *she* was going to bicycle.
Year after year, I had seen that famous Countess
riding or driving in the Park. I had been told at
fourth hand that she had a masculine intellect and
could make and unmake Ministries. She was nearly
sixty now, a trifle dyed and stout and weather-beaten,
but still tremendously handsome, and hard as nails.
One would not have said she had grown older, but
merely that she belonged now to a rather later period
of the Roman Empire. I had never dreamed of a time
when one roof would shelter Lady Rodfitten and me.
Somehow, she struck my imagination more than any
of these others—more than Count Deym, more than
Mr. Balfour, more than the lovely Lady Thisbe
Crowborough.

'I might have had a ducal vehicle all to myself, and
should have liked that; but it seemed more correct
that I should use my bicycle. On the other hand, I
didn't want to ride with all these people—a stranger
in their midst. I lingered around the luggage till they
were off, and then followed at a long distance.

'The sun had gone behind clouds. But I rode
slowly, so as to be sure not to arrive hot. I passed,
not without a thrill, through the massive open gates
into the Duke's park. A massive man with a cockade
saluted me—hearteningly—from the door of the
lodge. The park seemed endless. I came, at length,

to a long straight avenue of elms that were almost
blatantly immemorial. At the end of it was—well,
I felt like a gnat going to stay in a public building.

'If there had been turnstiles—IN and OUT—and
a shilling to pay, I should have felt easier as I passed
into that hall—that Palladio-Gargantuan hall. Some
one, some butler or groom-of-the-chamber, murmured that her Grace was in the garden. I passed
out through the great opposite doorway on to a wide
spectacular terrace with lawns beyond. Tea was on
the nearest of these lawns. In the central group of
people—some standing, others sitting—I espied the
Duchess. She sat pouring out tea, a deft and animated
little figure. I advanced firmly down the steps from
the terrace, feeling that all would be well so soon as
I had reported myself to the Duchess.

'But I had a staggering surprise on my way to her.
I espied in one of the smaller groups—whom d'you
think? Braxton.

'I had no time to wonder how he had got there—
time merely to grasp the black fact that he *was*
there.

'The Duchess seemed really pleased to see me.
She said it was *too* splendid of me to come. "You
know Mr. Maltby?" she asked Lady Rodfitten, who
exclaimed "Not Mr. *Hilary* Maltby?" with a
vigorous grace that was overwhelming. Lady Rodfitten declared she was the greatest of my admirers;
and I could well believe that in whatever she did she
excelled all competitors. On the other hand, I found
it hard to believe she was afraid of me. Yet I had her
word for it that she was.

'Her womanly charm gave place now to her masculine grip. She eulogised me in the language of a seasoned reviewer on the staff of a long-established journal—wordy perhaps, but sound. I revered and loved her. I wished I could give her my undivided attention. But, whilst I sat there, teacup in hand, between her and the Duchess, part of my brain was fearfully concerned with that glimpse I had had of Braxton. It didn't so much matter that he was here to halve my triumph. But suppose he knew what I had told the Duchess? And suppose he had—no, surely if he *had* shown me up in all my meanness she wouldn't have received me so very cordially. I wondered where she could have met him since that evening of the Inkwomen. I heard Lady Rodfitten concluding her review of "Ariel" with two or three sentences that might have been framed specially to give the publisher an easy "quote." And then I heard myself asking mechanically whether she had read "A Faun on the Cotswolds." The Duchess heard me too. She turned from talking to other people and said "I did like Mr. Braxton so *very* much."

'"Yes," I threw out with a sickly smile, "I'm so glad you asked him to come."

'"But I didn't ask him. I didn't *dare*."

'"But—but—surely he wouldn't be—be *here* if—" We stared at each other blankly. "Here?" she echoed, glancing at the scattered little groups of people on the lawn. I glanced too. I was much embarrassed. I explained that I had seen Braxton "standing just over there" when I arrived, and had supposed he was one of the people who came by the earlier train.

"Well," she said with a slightly irritated laugh, "you must have mistaken some one else for him." She dropped the subject, talked to other people, and presently moved away.

'Surely, thought I, she didn't suspect me of trying to make fun of her? On the other hand, surely she hadn't conspired with Braxton to make a fool of *me*? And yet, how could Braxton be here without an invitation, and without her knowledge? My brain whirled. One thing only was clear. I could *not* have mistaken anybody for Braxton. There Braxton had stood—Stephen Braxton, in that old pepper-and-salt suit of his, with his red tie all askew, and without a hat—his hair hanging over his forehead. All this I had seen sharp and clean-cut. There he had stood, just beside one of the women who travelled down in the same compartment as I; a very pretty woman in a pale blue dress; a tall woman—but I had noticed how small she looked beside Braxton. This woman was now walking to and fro, yonder, with M. de Soveral. I had seen Braxton beside her as clearly as I now saw M. de Soveral.

'Lady Rodfitten was talking about India to a recent Viceroy. She seemed to have as firm a grip of India as of "Ariel." I sat forgotten. I wanted to arise and wander off—in a vague search for Braxton. But I feared this might look as if I were angry at being ignored. Presently Lady Rodfitten herself arose, to have what she called her "annual look round." She bade me come too, and strode off between me and the recent Viceroy, noting improvements that had been made in the grounds, suggesting improvements that might be made, indicating improvements that *must* be made. She was great on landscape-gardening. The recent Viceroy was less great on it, but great enough. I don't say I walked forgotten: the eminent woman constantly asked my opinion; but my opinion, though of course it always coincided with hers, sounded quite worthless, somehow. I longed to shine. I could only bother about Braxton.

'Lady Rodfitten's voice was over-strong for the stillness of evening. The shadows lengthened. My spirits sank lower and lower, with the sun. I was a naturally cheerful person, but always, towards sunset, I had a vague sense of melancholy: I seemed always to have grown weaker; morbid misgivings would come to me. On this particular evening there was one such misgiving that crept in and out of me again and again . . . a very horrible misgiving as to the *nature* of what I had seen.

'Well, dressing for dinner is always great tonic. Especially if one shaves. My spirits rose as I lathered my face. I smiled to my reflection in the mirror. The afterglow of the sun came through the window behind the dressing-table, but I had switched on all the lights. My new silver-topped bottles and things made a fine array. To-night *I* was going to shine, too. I felt I might yet be the life and soul of the party. Anyway, my new evening suit was without a fault. And meanwhile this new razor was perfect. Having shaved "down," I lathered myself again and proceeded to shave "up." It was then that I uttered a sharp sound and swung round on my heel.

'No one was there. Yet this I knew: Stephen

Braxton had just looked over my shoulder. I had seen
the reflection of his face beside mine—craned forward to the mirror. I had met his eyes.

'He had been with me. This I knew.

'I turned to look again at that mirror. One of my
cheeks was all covered with blood. I stanched it with
a towel. Three long cuts where the razor had slipped
and skipped. I plunged the towel into cold water and
held it to my cheek. The bleeding went on—alarm-
ingly. I rang the bell. No one came. I vowed I
wouldn't bleed to death for Braxton. I rang again.
At last a very tall powdered footman appeared—
more reproachful-looking than sympathetic, as
though I hadn't ordered that dressing-case specially
on his behalf. He said he thought one of the housemaids would have some sticking-plaster. He was very
sorry he was needed downstairs, but he would tell
one of the housemaids. I continued to dab and to
curse. The blood flowed less. I showed great spirit.
I vowed Braxton should not prevent me from going
down to dinner.

'But—a pretty sight I was when I did go down.
Pale but determined, with three long strips of black
sticking-plaster forming a sort of Z on my left cheek.
Mr. Hilary Maltby at Keeb. Literature's Ambassador.

'I don't know how late I was. Dinner was in full
swing. Some servant piloted me to my place. I sat
down unobserved. The woman on either side of me
was talking to her other neighbour. I was near the
Duchess' end of the table. Soup was served to me—
that dark-red soup that you pour cream into—

Bortsch. I felt it would steady me. I raised the first spoonful to my lips, and—my hand gave a sudden jerk.

'I was aware of two separate horrors—a horror that had been, a horror that was. Braxton had vanished. Not for more than an instant had he stood scowling at me from behind the opposite diners. Not for more than the fraction of an instant. But he had left his mark on me. I gazed down with a frozen stare at my shirtfront, at my white waistcoat, both dark with Bortsch. I rubbed them with a napkin. I made them worse.

'I looked at my glass of champagne. I raised it carefully and drained it at one draught. It nerved me. But behind that shirtfront was a broken heart.

'The woman on my left was Lady Thisbe Crowborough. I don't know who was the woman on my right. She was the first to turn and see me. I thought it best to say something about my shirtfront at once. I said it to her sideways, without showing my left cheek. Her handsome eyes rested on the splashes. She said, after a moment's thought, that they looked "rather gay." She said she thought the eternal black and white of men's evening clothes was "so very dreary." She did her best. . . . Lady Thisbe Crowborough did her best, too, I suppose; but breeding isn't proof against all possible shocks: she visibly started at sight of me and my Z. I explained that I had cut myself shaving. I said, with an attempt at lightness, that shy men ought always to cut themselves shaving: it made such a good conversational opening. "But surely," she said after a pause, "you don't

cut yourself on purpose?'' She was an abysmal fool.
I didn't think so at the time. She was Lady Thisbe
Crowborough. This fact hallowed her. That we
didn't get on at all well was a misfortune for which
I blamed only myself and my repulsive appearance
and—the unforgettable horror that distracted me.
Nor did I blame Lady Thisbe for turning rather soon
to the man on her other side.

'The woman on my right was talking to the man
on *her* other side; so that I was left a prey to secret
memory and dread. I wasn't wondering, wasn't
attempting to explain; I was merely remembering—
and dreading. And—how odd one is!—on the top-
layer of my consciousness I hated to be seen talking
to no one. Mr. Maltby at Keeb. I caught the Duchess'
eye once or twice, and she nodded encouragingly, as
who should say "You do look rather awful, and you
do seem rather out of it, but I don't for a moment
regret having asked you to come." Presently I had
another chance of talking. I heard myself talk. My
feverish anxiety to please rather touched *me*. But I
noticed that the eyes of my listener wandered. And
yet I was sorry when the ladies went away. I had a
sense of greater exposure. Men who hadn't seen me
saw me now. The Duke, as he came round to the
Duchess' end of the table, must have wondered who
I was. But he shyly offered me his hand as he passed,
and said it was so good of me to come. I had thought
of slipping away to put on another shirt and waistcoat, but had decided that this would make me the
more ridiculous. I sat drinking port—poison to me
after champagne, but a lulling poison—and listened

to noblemen with unstained shirtfronts talking about the Australian cricket match. . . .

'Is Rubicon Bézique still played in England? There was a mania for it at that time. The floor of Keeb's Palladio-Gargantuan hall was dotted with innumerable little tables. I didn't know how to play. My hostess told me I must "come and amuse the dear old Duke and Duchess of Mull," and led me to a remote sofa on which an old gentleman had just sat down beside an old lady. They looked at me with a dim kind interest. My hostess had set me and left me on a small gilt chair in front of them. Before going she had conveyed to them loudly—one of them was very deaf—that I was "the famous writer." It was a long time before they understood that I was not a political writer. The Duke asked me, after a troubled pause, whether I had known "old Mr. Abraham Hayward." The Duchess said I was too young to have known Mr. Hayward, and asked if I knew her "clever friend Mr. Mallock." I said I had just been reading Mr. Mallock's new novel. I heard myself shouting a confused précis of the plot. The place where we were sitting was near the foot of the great marble staircase. I said how beautiful the staircase was. The Duchess of Mull said she had never cared very much for that staircase. The Duke, after a pause, said he had "often heard old Mr. Abraham Hayward hold a whole dinner table." There were long and frequent pauses—between which I heard myself talking loudly, frantically, sinking lower and lower in the esteem of my small audience. I felt like a man drowning under the eyes of an elderly couple who sit on the

bank regretting that they can offer *no* assistance.
Presently the Duke looked at his watch and said to
the Duchess that it was "time to be thinking of
bed."

'They rose, as it were from the bank, and left me,
so to speak, under water. I watched them as they
passed slowly out of sight up the marble staircase
which I had mispraised. I turned and surveyed
the brilliant, silent scene presented by the card-
players.

'I wondered what old Mr. Abraham Hayward
would have done in my place. Would he have just
darted in among those tables and "held" them?
I presumed that he would not have stolen silently
away, quickly and cravenly away, up the marble
staircase—as *I* did.

'I don't know which was the greater, the relief or
the humiliation of finding myself in my bedroom.
Perhaps the humiliation was the greater. There, on
a chair, was my grand new smoking-suit, laid out for
me—what a mockery! Once I had foreseen myself
wearing it in the smoking-room at a late hour—the
centre of a group of eminent men entranced by the
brilliancy of my conversation. And now—! I was
nothing but a small, dull, soup-stained, sticking-
plastered, nerve-racked recluse. Nerves, yes. I
assured myself that I had not seen—what I had
seemed to see. All very odd, of course, and very unpleasant, but easily explained. Nerves. Excitement
of coming to Keeb too much for me. A good night's
rest: that was all I needed. To-morrow I should
laugh at myself.

'I wondered that I wasn't tired physically. There my grand new silk pyjamas were, yet I felt no desire to go to bed . . . none while it was still possible for me to go. The little writing-table at the foot of my bed seemed to invite me. I had brought with me in my portmanteau a sheaf of letters, letters that I had purposely left unanswered in order that I might answer them on KEEB HALL note-paper. These the footman had neatly laid beside the blotting-pad on that little writing-table at the foot of the bed. I regretted that the note-paper stacked there had no ducal coronet on it. What matter? The address sufficed. If I hadn't yet made a good impression on the people who were staying here, I could at any rate make one on the people who weren't. I sat down. I set to work. I wrote a prodigious number of fluent and graceful notes.

'Some of these were to strangers who wanted my autograph. I was always delighted to send my autograph, and never perfunctory in the manner of sending it. . . . "Dear Madam," I remember writing to somebody that night, "Were it not that you make your request for it so charmingly, I should hesitate to send you that which rarity alone can render valuable.—Yours truly, Hilary Maltby." I remember reading this over and wondering whether the word "render" looked rather commercial. It was in the act of wondering thus that I raised my eyes from the note-paper and saw, through the bars of the brass bedstead, the naked sole of a large human foot—saw beyond it the calf of a great leg; a nightshirt; and the face of Stephen Braxton. I did not move.

'I thought of making a dash for the door, dashing out into the corridor, shouting at the top of my voice for help. I sat quite still.

'What kept me to my chair was the fear that if I tried to reach the door Braxton would spring off the bed to intercept me. If I sat quite still perhaps he wouldn't move. I felt that if he moved I should collapse utterly.

'I watched him, and he watched me. He lay there with his body half-raised, one elbow propped on the pillow, his jaw sunk on his breast; and from under his black brows he watched me steadily.

'No question of mere nerves now. That hope was gone. No mere optical delusion, this abiding presence. Here Braxton was. He and I were together in the bright, silent room. How long would he be content to watch me?

'Eleven nights ago he had given me one horrible look. It was this look that I had to meet, in infinite prolongation, now, not daring to shift my eyes. He lay as motionless as I sat. I did not hear him breathing, but I knew, by the rise and fall of his chest under his nightshirt, that he was breathing heavily. Suddenly I started to my feet. For he had moved. He had raised one hand slowly. He was stroking his chin. And as he did so, and as he watched me, his mouth gradually slackened to a grin. It was worse, it was more malign, this grin, than the scowl that remained with it; and its immediate effect on me was an impulse that was as hard to resist as it was hateful. The window was open. It was nearer to me than the door. I could have reached it in time. . . .

'Well, I live to tell the tale. I stood my ground.
And there dawned on me now a new fact in regard
to my companion. I had all the while been conscious
of something abnormal in his attitude—a lack of ease
in his gross possessiveness. I saw now the reason for
this effect. The pillow on which his elbow rested was
still uniformly puffed and convex; like a pillow un-
touched. His elbow rested but on the very surface of
it, not changing the shape of it at all. His body made
not the least furrow along the bed. . . . He had no
weight.

'I knew that if I leaned forward and thrust my
hand between those brass rails, to clutch his foot,
I should clutch—nothing. He wasn't tangible. He
was realistic. He wasn't real. He was opaque. He
wasn't solid.

'Odd as it may seem to you, these certainties took
the edge off my horror. During that walk with Lady
Rodfitten, I had been appalled by the doubt that
haunted me. But now the very confirmation of that
doubt gave me a sort of courage: I could cope better
with anything to-night than with actual Braxton.
And the measure of the relief I felt is that I sat down
again on my chair.

'More than once there came to me a wild hope that
the thing might be an optical delusion, after all.
Then would I shut my eyes tightly, shaking my head
sharply; but, when I looked again, there the presence was, of course. It—he—not actual Braxton
but, roughly speaking, Braxton—had come to stay.
I was conscious of intense fatigue, taut and alert
though every particle of me was; so that I became, in

the course of that ghastly night, conscious of a great
envy also. For some time before the dawn came in
through the window, Braxton's eyes had been closed;
little by little now his head drooped sideways, then
fell on his forearm and rested there. He was asleep.

'Cut off from sleep, I had a great longing for smoke.
I had cigarettes on me, I had matches on me. But
I didn't dare to strike a match. The sound might have
waked Braxton up. In slumber he was less terrible,
though perhaps more odious. I wasn't so much
afraid now as indignant. "It's intolerable," I sat saying to myself, "utterly intolerable!"

'I had to bear it, nevertheless. I was aware that
I had, in some degree, brought it on myself. If I
hadn't interfered and lied, actual Braxton would have
been here at Keeb, and I at this moment sleeping
soundly. But this was no excuse for Braxton.
Braxton didn't know what I had done. He was
merely envious of me. And—wanly I puzzled it out
in the dawn—by very force of the envy, hatred, and
malice in him he had projected hither into my presence this simulacrum of himself. I had known that
he would be thinking of me. I had known that the
thought of me at Keeb Hall would be of the last
bitterness to his most sacred feelings. But—I had
reckoned without the passionate force and intensity
of the man's nature.

'If by this same strength and intensity he had
merely projected himself as an invisible guest under
the Duchess' roof—if his feat had been wholly, as
perhaps it was in part, a feat of mere wistfulness and
longing—then I should have felt really sorry for

him; and my conscience would have soundly rated me in his behalf. But no; if the wretched creature *had* been invisible to me, I shouldn't have thought of Braxton at all—except with gladness that he wasn't here. That he was visible to me, and to me alone, wasn't any sign of proper remorse within me. It was but the gauge of his incredible ill-will.

'Well, it seemed to me that he was avenged—with a vengeance. There I sat, hot-browed from sleeplessness, cold in the feet, stiff in the legs, cowed and indignant all through—sat there in the broadening daylight, and in that new evening suit of mine with the Braxtonised shirtfront and waistcoat that by day were more than ever loathsome. Literature's Ambassador at Keeb. . . . I rose gingerly from my chair, and caught sight of my face, of my Braxtonised cheek, in the mirror. I heard the twittering of birds in distant trees. I saw through my window the elaborate landscape of the Duke's grounds, all soft in the grey bloom of early morning. I think I was nearer to tears than I had ever been since I was a child. But the weakness passed. I turned towards the personage on my bed, and, summoning all such power as was in me, *willed* him to be gone. My effort was not without result—an inadequate result. Braxton turned in his sleep.

'I resumed my seat, and . . . and . . . sat up staring and blinking at a tall man with red hair. "I must have fallen asleep," I said. "Yessir," he replied; and his toneless voice touched in me one or two springs of memory: I was at Keeb; this was the footman who looked after me. But—why wasn't I in bed? Had

I—no, surely it had been no nightmare. Surely I had
seen Braxton on that white bed.

'The footman was impassively putting away my
smoking-suit. I was too dazed to wonder what he
thought of me. Nor did I attempt to stifle a cry when,
a moment later, turning in my chair, I beheld
Braxton leaning moodily against the mantelpiece.
"Are you unwellsir?" asked the footman. "No,"
I said faintly, "I'm quite well."—"Yessir. Will you
wear the blue suit or the grey?"—"The grey."—
"Yessir."—It seemed almost incredible that *he* didn't
see Braxton; *he* didn't appear to me one whit more
solid than the night-shirted brute who stood against
the mantelpiece and watched him lay out my things.
—"Shall I let your bath-water run nowsir?"—
"Please, yes."—"Your bathroom's the second door
to the leftsir."—He went out with my bath-towel
and sponge, leaving me alone with Braxton.

'I rose to my feet, mustering once more all the
strength that was in me. Hoping against hope, with
set teeth and clenched hands, I faced him, thrust
forth my will at him, with everything but words commanded him to vanish—to cease to be.

'Suddenly, utterly, he vanished. And you can
imagine the truly exquisite sense of triumph that
thrilled me and continued to thrill me till I went
into the bathroom and found him in my bath.

'Quivering with rage, I returned to my bedroom.
"Intolerable," I heard myself repeating like a parrot
that knew no other word. A bath was just what I had
needed. Could I have lain for a long time basking in
very hot water, and then have sponged myself with

cold water, I should have emerged calm and brave; comparatively so, at any rate. I should have looked less ghastly, and have had less of a headache, and something of an appetite, when I went down to breakfast. Also, I shouldn't have been the very first guest to appear on the scene. There were five or six round tables, instead of last night's long table. At the further end of the room the butler and two other servants were lighting the little lamps under the hot dishes. I didn't like to make myself ridiculous by running away. On the other hand, was it right for me to begin breakfast all by myself at one of these round tables? I supposed it was. But I dreaded to be found eating, alone in that vast room, by the first down-comer. I sat dallying with dry toast and watching the door. It occurred to me that Braxton might occur at any moment. Should I be able to ignore him?

'Some man and wife—a very handsome couple— were the first to appear. They nodded and said "good morning" when they noticed me on their way to the hot dishes. I rose—uncomfortably, guiltily— and sat down again. I rose again when the wife drifted to my table, followed by the husband with two steaming plates. She asked me if it wasn't a heavenly morning, and I replied with nervous enthu-siasm that it was. She then ate kedgeree in silence. "You just finishing, what?" the husband asked, look-ing at my plate. "Oh, no—no—only just beginning," I assured him, and helped myself to butter. He then ate kedgeree in silence. He looked like some splendid bull, and she like some splendid cow, grazing. I envied them their eupeptic calm. I surmised that

ten thousand Braxtons would not have prevented
them from sleeping soundly by night and grazing
steadily by day. Perhaps their stolidity infected me
a little. Or perhaps what braced me was the great
quantity of strong tea that I consumed. Anyhow, I
had begun to feel that if Braxton came in now I
shouldn't blench nor falter.

'Well, I wasn't put to the test. Plenty of people
drifted in, but Braxton wasn't one of them. Lady
Rodfitten—no, she didn't drift, she marched, in;
and presently, at an adjacent table, she was drawing
a comparison, in clarion tones, between Jean and
Edouard de Reszke. It seemed to me that her own
voice had much in common with Edouard's. Even
more was it akin to a military band. I found myself
beating time to it with my foot. Decidedly, my spirits
had risen. I was in a mood to face and outface anything. When I rose from the table and made my way
to the door, I walked with something of a swing—to
the tune of Lady Rodfitten.

'My buoyancy didn't last long, though. There was
no swing in my walk when, a little later, I passed
out on to the spectacular terrace. I had seen my
enemy elsewhere, and had beaten a furious retreat.
No doubt I should see him yet again soon—here,
perhaps, on this terrace. Two of the guests were
bicycling slowly up and down the long paven expanse,
both of them smiling with pride in the new delicious
form of locomotion. There was a great array of
bicycles propped neatly along the balustrade. I recognised my own among them. I wondered whether
Braxton had projected from Clifford's Inn an image

of *his* own bicycle. He may have done so; but I've no evidence that he did. I myself was bicycling when next I saw him; he, I remember, was on foot.

'This was a few minutes later. I was bicycling with dear Lady Rodfitten. She seemed really to like me. She had come out and accosted me heartily on the terrace, asking me, because of my sticking-plaster, with whom I had fought a duel since yesterday. I did not tell her with whom, and she had already branched off on the subject of duelling in general. She regretted the extinction of duelling in England, and gave cogent reasons for her regret. Then she asked me what my next book was to be. I confided that I was writing a sort of sequel—"Ariel Returns to Mayfair." She shook her head, said with her usual soundness that sequels were very dangerous things, and asked me to tell her "briefly" the lines along which I was working. I did so. She pointed out two or three weak points in my scheme. She said she could judge better if I would let her see my manuscript. She asked me to come and lunch with her next Friday—"just our two selves"—at Rodfitten House, and to bring my manuscript with me. Need I say that I walked on air?

' "And now," she said strenuously, "let us take a turn on our bicycles." By this time there were a dozen riders on the terrace, all of them smiling with pride and rapture. We mounted and rode along together. The terrace ran round two sides of the house, and before we came to the end of it these words had provisionally marshalled themselves in my mind:

TO
ELEANOR
COUNTESS OF RODFITTEN
THIS BOOK WHICH OWES ALL
TO HER WISE COUNSEL
AND UNWEARYING SUPERVISION
IS GRATEFULLY DEDICATED
BY HER FRIEND
THE AUTHOR

'Smiled to masonically by the passing bicyclists, and smiling masonically to them in return, I began to feel that the rest of my visit would run smooth, if only——

'"Let's go a little faster. Let's race!" said Lady Rodfitten; and we did so—"just our two selves." I was on the side nearer to the balustrade, and it was on this side that Braxton suddenly appeared from nowhere, solid-looking as a rock, his arms akimbo, less than three yards ahead of me, so that I swerved involuntarily, sharply, striking broadside the front wheel of Lady Rodfitten and collapsing with her, and with a crash of machinery, to the ground.

'I wasn't hurt. She had broken my fall. I wished I was dead. She was furious. She sat speechless with fury. A crowd had quickly collected—just as in the case of a street accident. She accused me now to the crowd. She said I had done it on purpose. She said such terrible things of me that I think the crowd's sympathy must have veered towards me. She was assisted to her feet. I tried to be one of the assistants. "Don't let him come near me!" she thundered. I caught sight of Braxton on the fringe of the crowd, grinning at me. "It was all HIS fault," I madly cried, pointing at him. Everybody looked at Mr. Balfour, just behind whom Braxton was standing. There was a general murmur of surprise, in which I have no doubt Mr. Balfour joined. He gave a chárming, blank, deprecating smile. "I mean—I can't explain what I mean," I groaned. Lady Rodfitten moved away, refusing support, limping terribly, towards the house. The crowd followed her, solicitous. I stood helplessly, desperately, where I was.

'I stood an outlaw, a speck on the now empty terrace. Mechanically I picked up my straw hat, and wheeled the two bent bicycles to the balustrade. I suppose Mr. Balfour has a charming nature. For he presently came out again—on purpose, I am sure, to alleviate my misery. He told me that Lady Rodfitten had suffered no harm. He took me for a stroll up and down the terrace, talking thoughtfully and enchantingly about things in general. Then, having done his deed of mercy, this Good Samaritan went back into the house. My eyes followed him with gratitude; but I was still bleeding from wounds beyond his skill. I escaped down into the gardens. I wanted to see no one. Still more did I want to be seen by no one. I dreaded in every nerve of me my reappearance among those people. I walked ever faster and faster, to stifle thought; but in vain. Why hadn't I simply ridden *through* Braxton? I was aware of being now in the park, among great trees and undulations of wild green ground. But Nature did not achieve the task that Mr. Balfour had attempted; and my anguish was unassuaged.

'I paused to lean against a tree in the huge avenue that led to the huge hateful house. I leaned wondering whether the thought of re-entering that house were the more hateful because I should have to face my fellow-guests or because I should probably have to face Braxton. A church bell began ringing somewhere. And anon I was aware of another sound—a twitter of voices. A consignment of hatted and parasoled ladies was coming fast down the avenue. My first impulse was to dodge behind my tree. But I feared that I had been observed; so that what was left to me of self-respect compelled me to meet these ladies.

'The Duchess was among them. I had seen her from afar at breakfast, but not since. She carried a prayer-book, which she waved to me as I approached. I was a disastrous guest, but still a guest, and nothing could have been prettier than her smile. "Most of my men this week," she said, "are Pagans, and all the others have dispatch-boxes to go through—except the dear old Duke of Mull, who's a member of the Free Kirk. You're Pagan, of course?"

'I said—and indeed it was a heart-cry—that I should like very much to come to church. "If I shan't be in the way," I rather abjectly added. It didn't strike me that Braxton would try to intercept me. I don't know why, but it never occurred to me, as I walked briskly along beside the Duchess, that I should meet him so far from the house. The church was in a corner of the park, and the way to it was by a side path that branched off from the end of the avenue. A little way along, casting its shadow across the path, was a large oak. It was from behind this tree, when we came to it, that Braxton sprang suddenly forth and tripped me up with his foot.

'Absurd to be tripped up by the mere semblance of a foot? But remember, I was walking quickly, and the whole thing happened in a flash of time. It was inevitable that I should throw out my hands and come down headlong—just as though the obstacle had been as real as it looked. Down I came on palms and knee-caps, and up I scrambled, very much hurt and shaken and apologetic. "*Poor* Mr. Maltby! *Really*—!" the Duchess wailed for me in this latest of my mishaps. Some other lady chased my straw hat, which had bowled far ahead. Two others helped to brush me. They were all very kind, with a quaver of mirth in their concern for me. I looked furtively around for Braxton, but he was gone. The palms of my hands were abraded with gravel. The Duchess said I must on no account come to church *now*. I was utterly determined to reach that sanctuary. I marched firmly on with the Duchess. Come what might on the way, I wasn't going to be left out here. I was utterly bent on winning at least one respite.

'Well, I reached the little church without further molestation. To be there seemed almost too good to be true. The organ, just as we entered, sounded its first notes. The ladies rustled into the front pew. I, being the one male of the party, sat at the end of the pew, beside the Duchess. I couldn't help feeling that my position was a proud one. But I had gone through too much to take instant pleasure in it, and was beset by thoughts of what new horror might await me on the way back to the house. I hoped the Service would not be brief. The swelling and dwindling strains of the "voluntary" on the small organ were strangely soothing. I turned to give an almost feudal glance to the simple villagers in the pews behind, and saw a sight that cowed my soul.

'Braxton was coming up the aisle. He came slowly, casting a tourist's eye at the stained-glass windows on either side. Walking heavily, yet with no sound of boots on the pavement, he reached our pew. There, towering and glowering, he halted, as though demanding that we should make room for him. A moment later he edged sullenly into the pew. Instinctively I had sat tight back, drawing my knees aside, in a shudder of revulsion against contact. But Braxton did not push past me. What he did was to sit slowly and fully down on me.

'No, not down *on* me. Down *through* me——and around me. What befell me was not mere ghastly contact with the intangible. It was inclusion, envelopment, eclipse. What Braxton sat down on was not I, but the seat of the pew; and what he sat back against was not my face and chest, but the back of the pew. I didn't realise this at the moment. All I knew was a sudden black blotting-out of all things; an infinite and impenetrable darkness. I dimly conjectured that I was dead. What was wrong with me, in point of fact, was that my eyes, with the rest of me, were inside Braxton. You remember what a great hulking fellow Braxton was. I calculate that as we sat there my eyes were just beneath the roof of his mouth. Horrible!

'Out of the unfathomable depths of that pitch darkness, I could yet hear the "voluntary" swelling and dwindling, just as before. It was by this I knew now that I wasn't dead. And I suppose I must have craned my head forward, for I had a sudden glimpse of things—a close quick downward glimpse of a pepper-and-salt waistcoat and of two great hairy hands clasped across it. Then darkness again. Either I had drawn back my head, or Braxton had thrust his forward; I don't know which. "Are you all right?" the Duchess' voice whispered, and no doubt my face was ashen. "Quite," whispered my voice. But this pathetic monosyllable was the last gasp of the social instinct in me. Suddenly, as the "voluntary" swelled to its close, there was a great sharp shuffling noise. The congregation had risen to its feet, at the entry of choir and vicar. Braxton had risen, leaving me in daylight. I beheld his towering back. The Duchess, beside him, glanced round at me. But I could not, dared not, stand up into that presented back, into that great waiting darkness. I did but clutch my hat from beneath the seat and hurry distraught down the aisle, out through the porch, into the open air.

'Whither? To what goal? I didn't reason. I merely fled—like Orestes; fled like an automaton along the path we had come by. And was followed? Yes, yes. Glancing back across my shoulder, I saw that brute some twenty yards behind me, gaining on me. I broke into a sharper run. A few sickening moments later, he was beside me, scowling down into my face.

'I swerved, dodged, doubled on my tracks, but he was always at me. Now and again, for lack of breath, I halted, and he halted with me. And then, when I had got my wind, I would start running again, in the insane hope of escaping him. We came, by what twisting and turning course I know not, to the great avenue, and as I stood there in an agony of panting I had a dazed vision of the distant Hall. Really I had quite forgotten I was staying at the Duke of Hertfordshire's. But Braxton hadn't forgotten. He planted himself in front of me. He stood between me and the house.

'Faint though I was, I could almost have laughed. Good heavens! was *that* all he wanted: that I shouldn't go back there? Did he suppose I wanted to go back there—with *him*? Was I the Duke's prisoner on parole? What was there to prevent me from just walking off to the railway station? I turned to do so.

'He accompanied me on my way. I thought that when once I had passed through the lodge gates he might vanish, satisfied. But no, he didn't vanish. It was as though he suspected that if he let me out of his sight I should sneak back to the house. He arrived with me, this quiet companion of mine, at the little railway station. Evidently he meant to see me off. I learned from an elderly and solitary porter that the next train to London was the 4.3.

'Well, Braxton saw me off by the 4.3. I reflected, as I stepped up into an empty compartment, that it wasn't yet twenty-four hours ago since I, or some one like me, had alighted at that station.

'The guard blew his whistle; the engine shrieked, and the train jolted forward and away; but I did not lean out of the window to see the last of my attentive friend.

'Really not twenty-four hours ago? Not twenty-four years?'

Maltby paused in his narrative. 'Well, well,' he said, 'I don't want you to think I overrate the ordeal of my visit to Keeb. A man of stronger nerve than mine, and of greater resourcefulness, might have coped successfully with Braxton from first to last— might have stayed on till Monday, making a very favourable impression on every one all the while. Even as it was, even after my manifold failures and sudden flight, I don't say my position was impossible. I only say it seemed so to me. A man less sensitive than I, and less vain, might have cheered up after writing a letter of apology to his hostess, and have resumed his normal existence as though nothing very terrible had happened after all. I wrote a few lines to the Duchess that night; but I wrote amidst the pre-parations for my departure from England: I crossed the Channel next morning. Throughout that Sunday afternoon with Braxton at the Keeb railway station, pacing the desolate platform with him, waiting in the desolating waiting-room with him, I was numb to regrets, and was thinking of nothing but the 4.3. On the way to Victoria my brain worked and my soul wilted. Every incident in my stay at Keeb stood out clear to me; a dreadful, a hideous pattern. I had done for myself, so far as *those* people were concerned.

And now that I had sampled *them*, what cared I for others? "Too low for a hawk, too high for a buzzard." That homely old saying seemed to sum me up. And suppose I *could* still take pleasure in the company of my own old upper-middle class, how would that class regard me now? Gossip percolates. Little by little, I was sure, the story of my Keeb fiasco would leak down into the drawing-room of Mrs. Foster-Dugdale. I felt I could never hold up my head in any company where anything of that story was known. Are you quite sure you never heard anything?'

I assured Maltby that all I had known was the great bare fact of his having stayed at Keeb Hall.

'It's curious,' he reflected. 'It's a fine illustration of the loyalty of those people to one another. I suppose there was a general agreement for the Duchess' sake that nothing should be said about her queer guest. But even if I had dared hope to be so efficiently hushed up, I couldn't have not fled. I wanted to forget. I wanted to leap into some void, far away from all reminders. I leapt straight from Ryder Street into Vaule-la-Rochette, a place of which I had once heard that it was the least frequented seaside-resort in Europe. I leapt leaving no address—leapt telling my landlord that if a suit-case and a portmanteau arrived for me he could regard them, them and their contents, as his own for ever. I daresay the Duchess wrote me a kind little letter, forcing herself to express a vague hope that I would come again "some other time." I daresay Lady Rodfitten did *not* write reminding me of my promise to lunch on Friday and bring "Ariel Returns to Mayfair" with me. I left that

manuscript at Ryder Street; in my bedroom grate;
a shuffle of ashes. Not that I'd yet given up all
thought of writing. But I certainly wasn't going to
write now about the two things I most needed to
forget. I wasn't going to write about the British
aristocracy, nor about any kind of supernatural
presence. . . . I did write a novel—my last—while
I was at Vaule. "Mr. and Mrs. Robinson." Did you
ever come across a copy of it?'

I nodded gravely.

'Ah; I wasn't sure,' said Maltby, 'whether it was
ever published. A dreary affair, wasn't it? I knew a
great deal about suburban life. But—well, I suppose
one can't really understand what one doesn't love,
and one can't make good fun without real understanding. Besides, what chance of virtue is there for
a book written merely to distract the author's mind?
I had hoped to be healed by sea and sunshine and
solitude. These things were useless. The labour of
"Mr. and Mrs. Robinson" did help, a little. When
I had finished it, I thought I might as well send it off
to my publisher. He had given me a large sum of
money, down, after "Ariel," for my next book—so
large that I was rather loth to disgorge. In the note
I sent with the manuscript, I gave no address, and
asked that the proofs should be read in the office.
I didn't care whether the thing were published or not.
I knew it would be a dead failure if it were. What
mattered one more drop in the foaming cup of my
humiliation? I knew Braxton would grin and gloat.
I didn't mind even that.'

'Oh, well,' I said, 'Braxton was in no mood for

grinning and gloating. "The Drones" had already appeared.'

Maltby had never heard of 'The Drones'—which I myself had remembered only in the course of his disclosures. I explained to him that it was Braxton's second novel, and was by way of being a savage indictment of the British aristocracy; that it was written in the worst possible taste, but was so very dull that it fell utterly flat; that Braxton had forthwith taken, with all of what Maltby had called 'the passionate force and intensity of his nature,' to drink, and had presently gone under and not re-emerged.

Maltby gave signs of genuine, though not deep, emotion, and cited two or three of the finest passages from 'A Faun on the Cotswolds.' He even expressed a conviction that 'The Drones' must have been misjudged. He said he blamed himself more than ever for yielding to that bad impulse at that Soirée.

'And yet,' he mused, 'and yet, honestly, I can't find it in my heart to regret that I did yield. I can only wish that all had turned out as well, in the end, for Braxton as for me. I wish he could have won out, as I did, into a great and lasting felicity. For about a year after I had finished "Mr. and Mrs. Robinson" I wandered from place to place, trying to kill memory, shunning all places frequented by the English. At last I found myself in Lucca. Here, if anywhere, I thought, might a bruised and tormented spirit find gradual peace. I determined to move out of my hotel into some permanent lodging. Not for felicity, not for any complete restoration of self-respect, was I hoping; only for peace. A "mezzano" conducted me to a noble and ancient house, of which, he told me, the owner was anxious to let the first floor. It was in much disrepair, but even so seemed to me very cheap. According to the simple Luccan standard, I am rich. I took that first floor for a year, had it furbished up, and engaged two servants. My "padrona" inhabited the ground floor. From time to time she allowed me to visit her there. She was the Contessa Adriano-Rizzoli, the last of her line. She is the Contessa Adriano-Rizzoli-Maltby. We have been married fifteen years.'

Maltby looked at his watch and, rising, took tenderly from the table his great bunch of roses. 'She is a lineal descendant,' he said, 'of the Emperor Hadrian.'

JAMES PETHEL

JAMES PETHEL

September 17th, 1912

THOUGH seven years have gone by since the day when last I saw him, and though that day was but the morrow of my first meeting with him, I was shocked when I saw in my newspaper this morning the announcement of his sudden death.

I had formed, in the dim past, the habit of spending August in Dieppe. The place was less popular then than it is now. Some pleasant English people shared it with some pleasant French people. We used rather to resent the race-week—the third week of the month—as an intrusion on our privacy. We sneered as we read in the Paris edition of the *New York Herald* the names of the intruders. We disliked the nightly crush in the baccarat room of the Casino, and the croupiers' obvious excitement at the high play. I made a point of avoiding that room during that week, for the especial reason that the sight of serious, habitual gamblers has always filled me with a depression bordering on disgust. Most of the men, by some subtle stress of their ruling passion, have grown so monstrously fat, and most of the women so harrowingly thin. The rest of the women seem to be marked out for apoplexy, and the rest of the men to be wasting away. One feels that anything thrown at them would be either embedded or shattered, and

looks vainly among them for a person furnished with
the normal amount of flesh. Monsters they are, all
of them, to the eye (though I believe that many of
them have excellent moral qualities in private life);
but, just as in an American town one goes sooner or
later—goes against one's finer judgment, but somehow goes—into the dime-museum, so, year by year,
in Dieppe's race-week, there would be always one
evening when I drifted into the baccarat room. It
was on such an evening that I first saw the man
whose memory I here celebrate. My gaze was held
by him for the very reason that he would have passed
unnoticed elsewhere. He was conspicuous, not in
virtue of the mere fact that he was taking the bank
at the principal table, but because there was nothing
at all odd about him.

Between his lips was a cigar of moderate size.
Everything about him, except the amount of money
he had been winning, seemed moderate. Just as he
was neither fat nor thin, so had his face neither that
extreme pallor nor that extreme redness which be-
longs to the faces of seasoned gamblers: it was just
a clear pink. And his eyes had neither the unnatural
brightness nor the unnatural dullness of the eyes
around him: they were ordinarily clear eyes, of an
ordinary grey. His very age was moderate: a putative thirty-six, not more. ('Not less,' I would have
said in those days.) He assumed no air of non-
chalance. He did not deal out the cards as though they
bored him. But he had no look of grim concentration.
I noticed that the removal of his cigar from his
mouth made never the least difference to his face,

for he kept his lips pursed out as steadily as ever when he was not smoking. And this constant pursing of his lips seemed to denote just a pensive interest.

His bank was nearly done now. There were but a few cards left. Opposite to him was a welter of parti-coloured counters which the croupier had not yet had time to sort out and add to the rouleaux already made; there were also a fair accumulation of notes and several little stacks of gold. In all, not less than five hundred pounds, certainly. Happy banker! How easily had he won in a few minutes more than I, with utmost pains, could earn in many months! I wished I were he. His lucre seemed to insult me personally. I disliked him. And yet I hoped he would not take another bank. I hoped he would have the good sense to pocket his winnings and go home. Deliberately to risk the loss of all those riches would intensify the insult to myself.

'Messieurs, la banque est aux enchères!' There was some brisk bidding, while the croupier tore open and shuffled the two new packs. But it was as I feared: the gentleman whom I resented kept his place.

'Messieurs, la banque est faite. Quinze mille francs à la banque. Messieurs, les cartes passent! Messieurs, les cartes passent!'

Turning to go, I encountered a friend—one of the race-weekers, but in a sense a friend.

'Going to play?' I asked.

'Not while Jimmy Pethel's taking the bank,' he answered, with a laugh.

'Is that the man's name?'

'Yes. Don't you know him? I thought every one knew old Jimmy Pethel.'

I asked what there was so wonderful about 'old Jimmy Pethel' that every one should be supposed to know him.

'Oh, he's a great character. Has extraordinary luck. Always.'

I do not think my friend was versed in the pretty theory that good luck is the unconscious wisdom of them who in previous incarnations have been consciously wise. He was a member of the Stock Exchange, and I smiled as at a certain quaintness in his remark. I asked in what ways besides luck the 'great character' was manifested. Oh, well, Pethel had made a huge 'scoop' on the Stock Exchange when he was only twenty-three, and very soon doubled that, and doubled it again; then retired. He wasn't more than thirty-five now. And? Oh, well, he was a regular all-round sportsman—had gone after big game all over the world and had a good many narrow shaves. Great steeple-chaser, too. Rather settled down now. Lived in Leicestershire mostly. Had a big place there. Hunted five times a week. Still did an occasional flutter, though. Cleared eighty thousand in Mexicans last February. Wife had been a barmaid at Cambridge. Married her when he was nineteen. Thing seemed to have turned out quite well. Altogether, a great character.

Possibly, thought I. But my cursory friend, accustomed to quick transactions and to things accepted 'on the nod,' had not proved his case to my slower, more literary intelligence. It was to him,

however, that I owed, some minutes later, a chance
of testing his opinion. At the cry of 'Messieurs, la
banque est aux enchères' we looked round and saw
that the subject of our talk was preparing to rise from
his place. 'Now one can punt!' said Grierson (this
was my friend's name), and turned to the bureau at
which counters are for sale. 'If old Jimmy Pethel
punts,' he added, 'I shall just follow his luck.' But
this lodestar was not to be. While my friend was buying counters, and I wondering whether I too would
buy some, Pethel himself came up to the bureau.
With his lips no longer pursed, he had lost his air of
gravity, and looked younger. Behind him was an
attendant bearing a big wooden bowl—that plain
but romantic bowl supplied by the establishment
to a banker whose gains are too great to be pocketed.
He and Grierson greeted each other. He said he had
arrived in Dieppe this afternoon—was here for a day
or two. We were introduced. He spoke to me with
some *empressement*, saying he was a 'very great
admirer' of my work. I no longer disliked him. Grierson, armed with counters, had now darted away to
secure a place that had just been vacated. Pethel,
with a wave of his hand towards the tables, said,
'I suppose you never condescend to this sort of
thing?'

'Well——' I smiled indulgently.

'Awful waste of time,' he admitted.

I glanced down at the splendid mess of counters
and gold and notes that were now becoming, under
the swift fingers of the little man at the bureau, an
orderly array. I did not say aloud that it pleased me

to be, and to be seen, talking, on terms of equality, to a man who had won so much. I did not say how wonderful it seemed to me that he, whom I had watched just now with awe and with aversion, had all the while been a great admirer of my work. I did but say (again indulgently) that I supposed baccarat to be as good a way of wasting time as another.

'Ah, but you despise us all the same!' He added that he always envied men who had resources within themselves. I laughed lightly, to imply that it *was* very pleasant to have such resources, but that I didn't want to boast. And indeed, I had never, I vow, felt flimsier than when the little man at the bureau, naming a fabulous sum, asked its owner whether he would take the main part in notes of mille francs? cinq mille? dix mille? quoi? Had it been mine, I should have asked to have it all in five-franc pieces. Pethel took it in the most compendious form and crumpled it into a pocket. I asked if he were going to play any more to-night.

'Oh, later on,' he said. 'I want to get a little sea-air into my lungs now'; and he asked with a sort of breezy diffidence if I would go with him. I was glad to do so. It flashed across my mind that yonder on the terrace he might suddenly blurt out, 'I say, look here, don't think me awfully impertinent, but this money's no earthly use to me: I do wish you'd accept it, as a very small return for all the pleasure your work has given me, and . . . *There!* PLEASE! Not another word!'—all with such candour, delicacy, and genuine zeal that I should be unable to refuse. But I must not raise false hopes in my reader.

Nothing of the sort happened. Nothing of that sort ever does happen.

We were not long on the terrace. It was not a night on which you could stroll and talk: there was a wind against which you had to stagger, holding your hat on tightly and shouting such remarks as might occur to you. Against that wind acquaintance could make no headway. Yet I see now that despite that wind— or rather because of it—I ought already to have known Pethel a little better than I did when we presently sat down together inside the café of the Casino. There had been a point in our walk, or our stagger, when we paused to lean over the parapet, looking down at the black and driven sea. And Pethel had shouted that it would be great fun to be out in a sailing-boat to-night and that at one time he had been very fond of sailing.

As we took our seats in the café, he looked around him with boyish interest and pleasure. Then, squaring his arms on the little table, he asked me what I would drink. I protested that I was the host—a position which he, with the quick courtesy of the very rich, yielded to me at once. I feared he would ask for champagne, and was gladdened by his demand for water. 'Apollinaris? St. Galmier? Or what?' I asked. He preferred plain water. I felt bound to warn him that such water was never 'safe' in these places. He said he had often heard that, but would risk it. I remonstrated, but he was firm. 'Alors,' I told the waiter, 'pour Monsieur un verre d'eau fraîche, et pour moi un demi blonde.' Pethel asked me to tell him who every one was. I told him no one was any one in particular, and suggested that we should talk about ourselves. 'You mean,' he laughed, 'that you want to know who the devil I am?' I assured him that I had often heard of him. At this he was unaffectedly pleased. 'But,' I added, 'it's always more interesting to hear a man talked about by himself.' And indeed, since he had *not* handed his winnings over to me, I did hope he would at any rate give me some glimpses into that 'great character' of his. Full though his life had been, he seemed but like a rather clever schoolboy out on a holiday. I wanted to know more.

'That beer does look good,' he admitted when the waiter came back. I asked him to change his mind. But he shook his head, raised to his lips the tumbler of water that had been placed before him, and meditatively drank a deep draught. 'I never,' he then said, 'touch alcohol of any sort.' He looked solemn; but all men do look solemn when they speak of their own habits, whether positive or negative, and no matter how trivial; and so (though I had really no warrant for not supposing him a reclaimed drunkard) I dared ask him for what reason he abstained.

'When I say I *never* touch alcohol,' he said hastily, in a tone as of self-defence, 'I mean that I don't touch it often—or at any rate—well, I never touch it when I'm *gambling*, you know. It—it takes the edge off.'

His tone did make me suspicious. For a moment I wondered whether he had married the barmaid rather for what she symbolised than for what in herself she was. But no, surely not: he had been only nineteen years old. Nor in any way had he now—this steady, brisk, clear-eyed fellow—the aspect of one who had since fallen. 'The edge off the excitement?' I asked.

'Rather! Of course that sort of excitement seems awfully stupid to *you*. But—no use denying it—I do like a bit of a flutter—just occasionally, you know. And one has to be in trim for it. Suppose a man sat down dead drunk to a game of chance, what fun would it be for him? None. And it's only a question of degree. Soothe yourself ever so little with alcohol, and you don't get *quite* the full sensation of gambling. You do lose just a little something of the proper tremors before a coup, the proper throes during a coup, the proper thrill of joy or anguish after a coup. . . . You're bound to, you know,' he added, purposely making this bathos when he saw me smiling at the heights to which he had risen.

'And to-night,' I asked, remembering his prosaically pensive demeanour in taking the bank, 'were you feeling these throes and thrills to the utmost?'

He nodded.

'And you'll feel them again to-night?'

'I hope so.'

'I wonder you can stay away.'

'Oh, one gets a bit deadened after an hour or so. One needs to be freshened up. So long as I don't bore you——'

I laughed, and held out my cigarette-case. 'I rather wonder you smoke,' I murmured, after giving him a light. 'Nicotine's a sort of drug. Doesn't it soothe you? Don't you lose just a little something of the tremors and things?'

He looked at me gravely. 'By Jove,' he ejaculated, 'I never thought of that. Perhaps you're right. 'Pon my word, I must think that over.'

I wondered whether he were secretly laughing at me. Here was a man to whom (so I conceived, with an effort of the imagination) the loss or gain of a few hundred pounds could not matter. I told him I had spoken in jest. 'To give up tobacco might,' I said, 'intensify the pleasant agonies of a gambler staking his little all. But in your case—well, frankly, I don't see where the pleasant agonies come in.'

'You mean because I'm beastly rich?'

'Rich,' I amended.

'All depends on what you call rich. Besides, I'm not the sort of fellow who's content with 3 per cent. A couple of months ago—I tell you this in confidence—I risked practically all I had, in an Argentine deal.'

'And lost it?'

'No, as a matter of fact I made rather a good thing out of it. I did rather well last February, too. But there's no knowing the future. A few errors of judgment—a war here, a revolution there, a big strike somewhere else, and—' He blew a jet of smoke from his lips, and looked at me as at one whom he could trust to feel for him in a crash already come.

My sympathy lagged, and I stuck to the point of my inquiry. 'Meanwhile,' I suggested, 'and all the more because you aren't merely a rich man, but also an active taker of big risks, how can these tiny little baccarat risks give you so much emotion?'

'There you rather have me,' he laughed. 'I've often

wondered at that myself. I suppose,' he puzzled it out, 'I do a good lot of make-believe. While I'm playing a game like this game to-night, I *imagine* the stakes are huge, and I *imagine* I haven't another penny in the world.'

'Ah! So that with you it's always a life-and-death affair?'

He looked away. 'Oh, no, I don't say that.'

'Stupid phrase,' I admitted. 'But,' there was yet one point I would put to him, 'if you have extraordinary luck—always—'

'There's no such thing as luck.'

'No, strictly, I suppose, there isn't. But if in point of fact you always do win, then—well, surely, perfect luck driveth out fear?'

'Who ever said I always won?' he asked sharply.

I waved my hands and said, 'Oh, you have the reputation, you know, for extraordinary luck.'

'That isn't the same thing as always winning. Besides, I *haven't* extraordinary luck—never *have* had. Good heavens,' he exclaimed, 'if I thought I had any more chance of winning than of losing, I'd—I'd—'

'Never again set foot in that baccarat room to-night,' I soothingly suggested.

'Oh, baccarat be blowed! I wasn't thinking of baccarat. I was thinking of—oh, lots of things; baccarat included, yes.'

'What things?' I ventured to ask.

'What things?' He pushed back his chair, and 'Look here,' he said with a laugh, 'don't pretend I haven't been boring your head off with all this talk about myself. You've been too patient. I'm off. Shall I see you to-morrow? Perhaps you'd lunch with us to-morrow? It would be a great pleasure for my wife. We're at the Hôtel Royal.'

I said I should be most happy, and called the waiter; at sight of whom my friend said he had talked himself thirsty, and asked for another glass of water. He mentioned that he had brought his car over with him: his little daughter (by the news of whose existence I felt idiotically surprised) was very keen on motoring, and they were all three starting the day after to-morrow for 'a spin through France.' Afterwards, they were going to Switzerland, 'for some climbing.' Did I care about motoring? If so, we might go for a spin after luncheon, to Rouen or somewhere? He drank his glass of water, and, linking a friendly arm in mine, passed out with me into the corridor. He asked what I was writing now, and said that he looked to me to 'do something big, one of these days,' and that he was sure I had it 'in' me. This remark (though of course I pretended to be pleased by it) irritated me very much. It was destined, as you shall see, to irritate me very much more in recollection.

Yet was I glad he had asked me to luncheon. Glad because I liked him, glad because I dislike mysteries. Though you may think me very dense for not having thoroughly understood Pethel in the course of my first meeting with him, the fact is that I was only conscious, and that dimly, of something more in him than he had cared to reveal—some veil behind which perhaps lurked his right to the title so airily bestowed on him by Grierson. I assured myself, as I walked home, that if veil there were I should to-morrow find an eyelet.

But one's intuition when it is off duty seems always so much more powerful an engine than it does on active service; and next day, at sight of Pethel awaiting me outside his hotel, I became less confident. His, thought I, was a face which, for all its animation, would tell nothing—nothing, at any rate, that mattered. It expressed well enough that he was pleased to see me; but for the rest, I was reminded, it had a sort of frank inscrutability. Besides, it was at all points so very usual a face—a face that couldn't (so I then thought), even if it had leave to, betray connexion with a 'great character.' It was a strong face, certainly. But so are yours and mine.

And very fresh it looked, though, as he confessed, Pethel had sat up in 'that beastly baccarat room' till 5 a.m. I asked, had he lost? Yes, he had lost steadily for four hours (proudly he laid stress on this), but in the end—well (he admitted), he had won it all back 'and a bit more.' 'By the way,' he murmured as we were about to enter the hall, 'don't ever happen to mention to my wife what I told you about that Argentine deal. She's always rather nervous about— investments. I don't tell her about them. She's rather a nervous woman altogether, I'm sorry to say.'

This did not square with my preconception of her. Slave that I am to traditional imagery, I had figured her as 'flaunting,' as golden-haired, as haughty to most men but with a provocative smile across the

shoulder for some. Nor indeed did her husband's
words prevent me from the suspicion that my eyes
deceived me when anon I was presented to a very
pale small lady whose hair was rather white than grey.
And the 'little daughter'! This prodigy's hair was
as yet 'down,' but looked as if it might be up at any
moment: she was nearly as tall as her father, whom
she very much resembled in face and figure and
heartiness of handshake. Only after a rapid mental
calculation could I account for her. 'I must warn you,
she's in a great rage this morning,' said Pethel. 'Do
try to soothe her.' She blushed, laughed, and bade
her father not be so silly. I asked her the cause of her
great rage. She said 'He only means I was disappointed. And he was just as disappointed as I was.
Weren't you, now, Father?'

'I suppose they meant well, Peggy,' he laughed.

'They were *quite* right,' said Mrs. Pethel, evidently not for the first time.

'They,' as I presently learned, were the authorities
of the bathing establishment. Pethel had promised
his daughter he would take her for a swim; but on
their arrival at the bathing-cabins they were ruth-
lessly told that bathing was 'défendu à cause du
mauvais temps.' This embargo was our theme as we
sat down to luncheon. Miss Peggy was of opinion that
the French were cowards. I pleaded for them that
even in English watering-places bathing was for-
bidden when the sea was *very* rough. She did not
admit that the sea was very rough to-day. Besides,
she appealed to me, what was the fun of swimming
in absolutely calm water? I dared not say that this

was the only sort of water I liked to swim in. 'They were *quite* right,' said Mrs. Pethel yet again.

'Yes, but, darling Mother, you can't swim. Father and I are both splendid swimmers.'

To gloze over the mother's disability, I looked brightly at Pethel, as though in ardent recognition of his prowess among waves. With a movement of his head he indicated his daughter—indicated that there was no one like her in the whole world. I beamed agreement. Indeed, I did think her rather nice. If one liked the father (and I liked Pethel all the more in that capacity), one couldn't help liking the daughter: the two were so absurdly alike. Whenever he was looking at her (and it was seldom that he looked away from her) the effect, if you cared to be fantastic, was that of a very vain man before a mirror. It might have occurred to me that, if there were any mystery in him, I could solve it through her. But, in point of fact, I had forgotten all about that possible mystery. The amateur detective was lost in the sympathetic observer of a father's love. That Pethel did love his daughter I have never doubted. One passion is not less true because another predominates. No one who ever saw that father with that daughter could doubt that he loved her intensely. And this intensity gauges for me the strength of what else was in him.

Mrs. Pethel's love, though less explicit, was not less evidently profound. But the maternal instinct is less attractive to an onlooker, because he takes it more for granted, than the paternal. What endeared poor Mrs. Pethel to me was—well, the inevitability of the epithet I give her. She seemed poor thing, so essentially out of it; and by 'it' is meant the glowing mutual affinity of husband and child. Not that she didn't, in her little way, assert herself during the meal. But she did so, I thought, with the knowledge that she didn't count, and never would count. I wondered how it was that she had, in that Cambridge bar-room long ago, counted for Pethel to the extent of matrimony. But from any such room she seemed so utterly remote that she might well be in all respects now an utterly changed woman. She did pre-eminently look as if much had by some means been taken out of her, with no compensatory process of putting in. Pethel looked so very young for his age, whereas she would have had to be quite old to look young for hers. I pitied her as one might a governess with two charges who were hopelessly out of hand. But a governess, I reflected, can always give notice. Love tied poor Mrs. Pethel fast to her present situation.

As the three of them were to start next day on their tour through France, and as the four of us were to make a tour to Rouen this afternoon, the talk was much about motoring—a theme which Miss Peggy's enthusiasm made almost tolerable. I said to Mrs. Pethel, with more good-will than truth, that I sup-posed she was 'very keen on it.' She replied that she was.

'But, darling Mother, you aren't. I believe you *hate* it. You're *always* asking Father to go slower. And what *is* the fun of just crawling along?'

'Oh, come, Peggy, we never crawl,' said her father.

'No, indeed,' said her mother, in a tone of which Pethel laughingly said it would put me off coming out with them this afternoon. I said, with an expert air to reassure Mrs. Pethel, that it wasn't fast driving, but only bad driving, that was a danger. 'There, Mother!' cried Peggy. 'Isn't that what we're always telling you?'

I felt that they were always either telling Mrs. Pethel something or, as in the matter of that intended bath, not telling her something. It seemed to me possible that Peggy advised her father about his 'investments.' I wondered whether they had yet told Mrs. Pethel of their intention to go on to Switzerland for some climbing.

Of his secretiveness for his wife's sake I had a touching little instance after luncheon. We had adjourned to have coffee in front of the hotel. The car was already in attendance, and Peggy had darted off to make her daily inspection of it. Pethel had given me a cigar, and his wife presently noticed that he himself was not smoking. He explained to her that he thought he had smoked too much lately, and that he was going to 'knock it off' for a while. I would not have smiled if he had met my eye. But his avoidance of it made me quite sure that he really had been 'thinking over' what I had said last night about nicotine and its possibly deleterious action on the gambling thrill.

Mrs. Pethel saw the smile that I could not repress. I explained that I was wishing *I* could knock off tobacco, and envying her husband's strength of character. She smiled too, but wanly, with her eyes on him. 'Nobody has so much strength of character as *he* has,' she said.

'Nonsense!' he laughed. 'I'm the weakest of men.'

'Yes,' she said quietly. 'That's true, too, James.'

Again he laughed, but he flushed. I saw that Mrs. Pethel also had faintly flushed; and I became horribly conscious of following suit. In the sudden glow and silence created by Mrs. Pethel's paradox, I was grateful to the daughter for bouncing back into our midst and asking how soon we should be ready to start.

Pethel looked at his wife, who looked at me and rather strangely asked if I were sure I wanted to go with them. I protested that of course I did. Pethel asked her if *she* really wanted to come: 'You see, dear, there was the run yesterday from Calais. And to-morrow you'll be on the road again, and all the days after.'

'Yes,' said Peggy, 'I'm *sure* you'd much rather stay at home, darling Mother, and have a good rest.'

'Shall we go and put on our things, Peggy?' replied Mrs. Pethel, rising from her chair. She asked her husband whether he were taking the chauffeur with him. He said he thought not.

'Oh, hurrah!' cried Peggy. 'Then I can be on the front seat!'

'No, dear,' said her mother. 'I am sure Mr. Beerbohm would like to be on the front seat.'

'You'd like to be with Mother, wouldn't you?' the girl appealed. I replied with all possible emphasis that I should like to be with Mrs. Pethel. But presently, when the mother and daughter reappeared in the guise of motorists, it became clear that my aspiration had been set aside. 'I am to be with Mother,' said Peggy.

I was inwardly glad that Mrs. Pethel could, after all, assert herself to some purpose. Had I thought she disliked me, I should have been hurt; but I was sure her desire that I should not sit with her was due merely to a belief that a person on the front seat was less safe in case of accidents than a person behind. And of course I did not expect her to prefer my life to her daughter's. Poor lady! My heart was with her. As the car glided along the sea-front and then under the Norman archway, through the town and past the environs, I wished that her husband inspired in her as much confidence as he did in me. For me the sight of his clear, firm profile (he did not wear motor-goggles) was an assurance in itself. From time to time (for I too was ungoggled) I looked round to nod and smile cheerfully at his wife. She always returned the nod, but left the smile to be returned by the daughter.

Pethel, like the good driver he was, did not talk: just drove. But he did, as we came out on to the Rouen road, say that in France he always rather missed the British police-traps. 'Not,' he added, 'that I've ever fallen into one. But the chance that a police-man *may* at any moment dart out, and land you in a bit of a scrape, does rather add to the excitement, don't you think?' Though I answered in the tone of one to whom the chance of a police-trap is the very salt of life, I did not inwardly like the spirit of his remark. However, I dismissed it from my mind; and the sun was shining, and the wind had dropped: it

was an ideal day for motoring; and the Norman landscape had never looked lovelier to me in its width of
sober and silvery grace.

I presently felt that this landscape was not, after
all, doing itself full justice. Was it not rushing rather
too quickly past? 'James!' said a shrill, faint voice
from behind; and gradually—'Oh, darling Mother,
really!' protested another voice—the landscape
slackened pace. But after a while, little by little, the
landscape lost patience, forgot its good manners, and
flew faster, and faster than before. The road rushed
furiously beneath us, like a river in spate. Avenues
of poplars flashed past us, every tree of them on either
side hissing and swishing angrily in the draught we
made. Motors going Rouen-wards seemed to be past
as quickly as motors that bore down on us. Hardly
had I espied in the landscape ahead a château or other
object of interest before I was craning my neck
round for a final glimpse of it as it faded on the back-
ward horizon. An endless up-hill road was breasted
and crested in a twinkling and transformed into a
decline near the end of which our car lept straight
across to the opposite ascent, and—'James!' again,
and again by degrees the laws of Nature were re-
established, but again by degrees revoked. I didn't
doubt that speed in itself was no danger; but when
the road was about to make a sharp curve why
shouldn't Pethel, just as a matter of form, slow down
slightly and sound a note or two of the hooter? Suppose another car were—well, that was all right: the
road was clear. But at the next turning, when our
car neither slackened nor hooted and *was*, for an

instant, full on the wrong side of the road, I had within me a contraction which (at thought of what must have been if——) lasted though all was well. Loth to betray fear, I hadn't turned my face to Pethel. Eyes front! And how about that wagon ahead, huge hay-wagon plodding with its back to us, seeming to occupy whole road? Surely Pethel would slacken, hoot? No. Imagine a needle threaded with one swift gesture from afar. Even so was it that we shot, between wagon and road's edge, through; whereon, confronting us within a few yards—inches now, but we swerved—was a cart, a cart that incredibly we grazed not as we rushed on, on. Now indeed had I turned my eyes on Pethel's profile. And my eyes saw there that which stilled, with a greater emotion, all fear and wonder in me.

I think that for the first instant, oddly, what I felt was merely satisfaction, not hatred; for I all but asked him whether by not smoking to-day he had got a keener edge to his thrills. I understood him, and for an instant this sufficed me. Those pursed-out lips, so queerly different from the compressed lips of the normal motorist, and seeming, as elsewhere last night, to denote no more than a pensive interest, had told me suddenly all that I needed to know about Pethel. Here, as there—and oh, ever so much better here than there!—he could gratify the passion that was in him. No need of any 'make-believe' here! I remembered the strange look he had given when I asked if his gambling were always 'a life-and-death affair.' Here was the real thing—the authentic game, for the highest stakes! And here was I, a little extra-stake tossed on to the board. He had vowed I had it 'in' me to do 'something big.' Perhaps, though, there had been a touch of his make-believe about that. . . . I am afraid it was not before my thought about myself that my moral sense began to operate and my hatred of Pethel set in. But I claim that I did see myself as no more than a mere detail in his villainy. Nor, in my just wrath for other sakes, was I without charity even for him. I gave him due credit for risking his own life—for having doubtless risked it, it and none other, again and again in the course of his adventurous—and abstemious—life by field and flood. I was even rather touched by memory of his insistence last night on another glass of that water which just *might* give him typhoid; rather touched by memory of his unsaying that he 'never' touched alcohol—he who, in point of fact, had to be *always* gambling on something or other. I gave him due credit, too, for his devotion to his daughter. But his use of that devotion, his cold use of it to secure for himself the utmost thrill of gambling, did seem utterly abominable to me.

And it was even more for the mother than for the daughter that I was incensed. That daughter did not know him, did but innocently share his damnable love of chances. But that wife had for years known him at least as well as I knew him now. Here again, I gave him credit for wishing, though he didn't love her, to spare her what he could. That he didn't love her I presumed from his indubitable willingness not to stake her in this afternoon's game. That he never had loved her—had taken her, in his precocious youth, simply as a gigantic chance against him—was likely enough. So much the more credit to him for such consideration as he showed her; but little enough this was. He could wish to save her from being a looker-on at his game; but he could, he couldn't not, go on playing. Assuredly she was right in deeming him at once the strongest and the weakest of men. 'Rather a nervous woman'! I remembered an engraving that had hung in my room at Oxford—and in scores of other rooms there: a presentment by Sir Marcus (then Mr.) Stone of a very pretty young person in a Gainsborough hat, seated beneath an ancestral elm, looking as though she were about to cry, and entitled 'A Gambler's Wife.' Mrs. Pethel was not like that. Of her there were no engravings for undergraduate hearts to melt at. But there was one man, certainly, whose compassion was very much at her service. How was he going to help her?

I know not how many hair's-breadth escapes we may have had while these thoughts passed through my brain. I had closed my eyes. So preoccupied was I that, but for the constant rush of air against my face, I might, for aught I knew, have been sitting ensconced in an arm-chair at home. After a while, I was aware that this rush had abated; I opened my eyes to the old familiar streets of Rouen. We were to have tea at the Hôtel d'Angleterre. What was to be my line of action? Should I take Pethel aside and say 'Swear to me, on your word of honour as a gentleman, that you will never again touch the driving-gear (or whatever you call it) of a motor-car. Otherwise I shall expose you to the world. Meanwhile, we shall return to Dieppe by train'? He might flush—for I knew him capable of flushing—as he asked me to explain. And after? He would laugh in my face. He would advise me not to go motoring any more. He might even warn me not to go back to Dieppe in one of those dangerous railway-trains. He might even urge me to wait until a nice Bath chair had been sent out for me from England. . . .

I heard a voice (mine, alas) saying brightly 'Well, here we are!' I helped the ladies to descend. Tea was ordered. Pethel refused that stimulant and had a glass of water. I had a liqueur brandy. It was evident to me that tea meant much to Mrs. Pethel. She looked stronger after her second cup, and younger after her third. Still, it was my duty to help her, if I could. While I talked and laughed, I did not forget that. But—what on earth was I to do? I am no hero. I hate to be ridiculous. I am inverately averse from any sort of fuss. Besides, how was I to be sure that my own personal dread of the return-journey hadn't something to do with my intention of tackling Pethel? I thought it had. What this woman would dare daily because she was a mother, could not I dare once? I reminded myself of Pethel's reputation for invariable luck. I reminded myself that he was an extraordinarily skilful driver. To that skill and luck I would pin my faith. . . .

What I seem to myself, do you ask of me? But I answered your question a few lines back. Enough that my faith was rewarded. We did reach Dieppe safely. I still marvel that we did.

That evening, in the vestibule of the Casino,

Grierson came up to me: 'Seen Jimmy Pethel? He was asking for you. Wants to see you particularly. He's in the baccarat room, punting—winning hand over fist, *of* course. Said he'd seldom met a man he liked more than you. Great character, what?' One is always glad to be liked, and I plead guilty to a moment's gratification at the announcement that Pethel liked me. But I did not go and seek him in the baccarat room. A great character assuredly he was; but of a kind with which (very imperfect though I am, and no censor) I prefer not to associate.

Why he had particularly wanted to see me was made clear in a note sent by him to my room early next morning. He wondered if I could be induced to join them in their little tour. He hoped I wouldn't think it great cheek, his asking me. He thought it might rather amuse me to come. It would be a very great pleasure for his wife. He hoped I wouldn't say No. Would I send a line by bearer? They would be starting at 3 o'clock. He was mine sincerely.

It was not too late to tackle him, even now. Should I go round to his hotel? I hesitated and—well, I told you at the outset that my last meeting with him was on the morrow of my first. I forget what I wrote to him, but am sure the excuse that I made for myself was a good and graceful one, and that I sent my kindest regards to Mrs. Pethel. She had not (I am sure of that, too) authorised her husband to say she would like me to come with them. Else would not the thought of her have haunted me so poignantly as for a long time it did. I do not know whether she is still alive. No mention is made of her in the obituary notice which woke these memories in me. This notice I will, however, transcribe, because (for all its crudeness of phraseology) it is rather interesting both as an echo and as an amplification. Its title is—'Death of Wealthy Aviator.' Its text is—'Widespread regret will be felt in Leicestershire at the tragic death of Mr. James Pethel, who had long resided there and was very popular as an all-round sportsman. In recent years he had been much interested in aviation, and had become one of the most enthusiastic of amateur airmen. Yesterday afternoon he fell down dead quite suddenly as he was returning to his house, apparently in his usual health and spirits, after descending from a short flight which despite an extremely high wind he had made on his new biplane and on which he was accompanied by his married daughter and her infant son. It is not expected that an inquest will be necessary, as his physician, Dr. Saunders, has certified death to be due to heart-disease, from which, it appears, the deceased gentleman had been suffering for some years. Dr. Saunders adds that he had repeatedly warned deceased that any strain on the nervous system might prove fatal.'

Thus—for I presume that his ailment had its origin in his habits—James Pethel did not, despite that merely pensive look of his, live his life with impunity. And by reason of that life he died. As for the manner of his death, enough that he did die. Let not our hearts be vexed that his great luck was with him to the end.

A. V. LAIDER

A. V. LAIDER

1914

I UNPACKED my things and went down to await luncheon.

It was good to be here again in this little old sleepy hostel by the sea. Hostel I say, though it spelt itself without an s and even placed a circumflex above the o. It made no other pretension. It was very cosy indeed.

I had been here just a year before, in mid-February, after an attack of influenza. And now I had returned, after an attack of influenza. Nothing was changed. It had been raining when I left, and the waiter—there was but a single, a very old waiter—had told me it was only a shower. That waiter was still here, not a day older. And the shower had not ceased.

Steadfastly it fell on to the sands, steadfastly into the iron-grey sea. I stood looking out at it from the windows of the hall, admiring it very much. There seemed to be little else to do. What little there was I did. I mastered the contents of a blue hand-bill which, pinned to the wall just beneath the framed engraving of Queen Victoria's Coronation, gave token of a concert that was to be held—or rather, was to have been held some weeks ago—in the Town Hall, for the benefit of the Life-Boat Fund. I looked at the barometer, tapped it, was not the wiser. I glanced at a pamphlet about Our Dying Industries (a theme on which Mr. Joseph Chamberlain was at that time trying to alarm us). I wandered to the letter-board.

These letter-boards always fascinate me. Usually some two or three of the envelopes stuck into the cross-garterings have a certain newness and freshness. They seem sure they will yet be claimed. Why not? Why *shouldn't* John Doe, Esq., or Mrs. Richard Roe, turn up at any moment? I do not know. I can only say that nothing in the world seems to me more unlikely. Thus it is that these young bright envelopes touch my heart even more than do their dusty and sallow seniors. Sour resignation is less touching than impatience for what will not be, than the eagerness that has to wane and wither. Soured beyond measure these old envelopes are. They are not nearly so nice as they should be to the young ones. They lose no chance of sneering and discouraging. Such dialogues as this are only too frequent:

A VERY YOUNG ENVELOPE. Something in me whispers that he will come to-day!

A VERY OLD ENVELOPE. He? Well, that's good! Ha, ha, ha! Why didn't he come last week, when *you* came? What reason have your for supposing he'll ever come *now*? It isn't as if he were a frequenter of the place. He's never been here. His name is utterly unknown here. You don't suppose he's coming on the chance of finding *you*?

A. V. Y. E. It may seem silly, but—something in me whispers——

A. V. O. E. Something in *you*? One has only to look at you to see there's nothing in you but a note scribbled to him by a cousin. Look at *me*! There are three sheets, closely written, in *me*. The lady to whom I am addressed——

A. V. Y. E. Yes, sir, yes; you told me all about her yesterday.

A. V. O. E. And I shall do so to-day and to-morrow and every day and all day long. That young lady was a widow. She stayed here many times. She was delicate, and the air suited her. She was poor, and the tariff was just within her means. She was lonely, and had need of love. I have in me for her a passionate avowal and strictly honourable proposal, written to her, after many rough copies, by a gentleman who had made her acquaintance under this very roof. He was rich, he was charming, he was in the prime of life. He had asked if he might write to her. She had flutteringly granted his request. He posted me to her the day after his return to London. I looked forward to being torn open by her. I was very sure she would wear me and my contents next to her bosom. She was gone. She had left no address. She never returned. . . . This I tell you, and shall continue to tell you, not because I want any of your callow sympathy,—no, *thank* you! —but that you may judge how much less than slight are the chances that you yourself——

But my reader has overheard these dialogues as often as I. He wants to know what was odd about this particular letter-board before which I was standing. At first glance I saw nothing odd about it. But presently I distinguished a handwriting that was vaguely familiar. It was mine. I stared, I wondered. There is always a slight shock in seeing an envelope of one's own after it has gone through the post. It looks as if it had gone through so much. But this was the first time I had ever seen an envelope of mine eating its heart out in bondage on a letter-board. This was outrageous. This was hardly to be believed. Sheer kindness had impelled me to write to 'A. V. Laider, Esq.', and this was the result! I hadn't minded receiving no answer. Only now, indeed, did I remember that I hadn't received one. In multitudinous London the memory of A. V. Laider and his trouble had soon passed from my mind. But—well, what a lesson not to go out of one's way to write to casual acquaintances!

My envelope seemed not to recognise me as its writer. Its gaze was the more piteous for being blank. Even so had I once been gazed at by a dog that I had lost and, after many days, found in the Battersea Home. 'I don't know who you are, but, whoever you are, claim me, take me out of this!' That was my dog's appeal. This was the appeal of my envelope.

I raised my hand to the letter-board, meaning to effect a swift and lawless rescue, but paused at sound of a footstep behind me. The old waiter had come to tell me that my luncheon was ready. I followed him out of the hall, not, however, without a bright glance across my shoulder to reassure the little captive that I should come back.

I had the sharp appetite of the convalescent, and this the sea-air had whetted already to a finer edge. In touch with a dozen oysters, and with stout, I soon shed away the unreasoning anger I had felt against A. V. Laider. I became merely sorry for him that he had not received a letter which might perhaps have comforted him. In touch with cutlets, I felt how sorely he had needed comfort. And anon, by the big bright fireside of that small dark smoking-room where, a year ago, on the last evening of my stay here, he and I had at length spoken to each other, I reviewed in detail the tragic experience he had told me: and I fairly revelled in reminiscent sympathy with him. . . .

A. V. LAIDER—I had looked him up in the visitors' book on the night of his arrival. I myself had arrived the day before, and had been rather sorry there was no one else staying here. A convalescent by the sea likes to have some one to observe, to wonder about, at meal-time. I was glad when, on my second evening, I found seated at the table opposite to mine another guest. I was the gladder because he was just the right kind of guest. He was enigmatic. By this I mean that he did not look soldierly nor financial nor artistic nor anything definite at all. He offered a clean slate for speculation. And thank heaven! he evidently wasn't going to spoil the fun by engaging me in conversation later on. A decently unsociable man, anxious to be left alone.

The heartiness of his appetite, in contrast with his extreme fragility of aspect and limpness of demeanour, assured me that he, too, had just had influenza. I liked him for that. Now and again our eyes met and were instantly parted. We managed, as a rule, to observe each other indirectly. I was sure it was not merely because he had been ill that he looked interesting. Nor did it seem to me that a spiritual melancholy, though I imagined him sad at the best of

times, was his sole asset. I conjectured that he was
clever. I thought he might also be imaginative. At
first glance I had mistrusted him. A shock of white
hair, combined with a young face and dark eyebrows,
does somehow make a man look like a charlatan. But
it is foolish to be guided by an accident of colour.
I had soon rejected my first impression of my fellow-
diner. I found him very sympathetic.

Anywhere but in England it would be impossible
for two solitary men, howsoever much reduced by
influenza, to spend five or six days in the same hostel
and not exchange a single word. That is one of the
charms of England. Had Laider and I been born
and bred in any other land we should have become
acquainted before the end of our first evening in the
small smoking-room, and have found ourselves irrevocably committed to go on talking to each other
throughout the rest of our visit. We might, it is true,
have happened to like each other more than any one
we had ever met. This off-chance may have occurred
to us both. But it counted for nothing as against the
certain surrender of quietude and liberty. We slightly
bowed to each other as we entered or left the dining-
room or smoking-room, and as we met on the widespread sands or in the shop that had a small and faded
circulating library. That was all. Our mutual aloofness was a positive bond between us.

Had he been much older than I, the responsibility
for our silence would of course have been his alone.
But he was not, I judged, more than five or six years
ahead of me, and thus I might without impropriety
have taken it on myself to perform that hard and

perilous feat which English people call, with a shiver,
'breaking the ice.' He had reason, therefore, to be as
grateful to me as I to him. Each of us, not the less
frankly because silently, recognised his obligation to
the other. And when, on the last evening of my stay,
the ice actually was broken no ill-will rose between us:
neither of us was to blame.

It was a Sunday evening. I had been out for a long
last walk and had come in very late to dinner. Laider
left his table almost immediately after I sat down to
mine. When I entered the smoking-room I found him
reading a weekly review which I had bought the day
before. It was a crisis. He could not silently offer,
nor could I have silently accepted, sixpence. It was
a crisis. We faced it like men. He made, by word of
mouth, a graceful apology. Verbally, not by signs,
I besought him to go on reading. But this, of course,
was a vain counsel of perfection. The social code
forced us to talk now. We obeyed it like men. To
reassure him that our position was not so desperate
as it might seem, I took the earliest opportunity to
mention that I was going away early next morning.
In the tone of his 'Oh, are you?' he tried bravely to
imply that he was sorry, even now, to hear that. In
a way, perhaps, he really was sorry. We had got on
so well together, he and I. Nothing could efface the
memory of that. Nay, we seemed to be hitting it off
even now. Influenza was not our sole theme. We
passed from that to the aforesaid weekly review, and
to a correspondence that was raging therein on Faith
and Reason.

This correspondence had now reached its fourth

and penultimate stage—its Australian stage. It is
hard to see why these correspondences spring up;
one only knows that they do spring up, suddenly,
like street crowds. There comes, it would seem, a
moment when the whole English-speaking race is
unconsciously bursting to have its say about some
one thing—the split infinitive, or the habits of mi-
gratory birds, or faith and reason, or what-not.
Whatever weekly review happens at such a moment
to contain a reference, however remote, to the theme
in question reaps the storm. Gusts of letters blow in
from all corners of the British Isles. These are
presently reinforced by Canada in full blast. A few
weeks later the Anglo-Indians weigh in. In due
course we have the help of our Australian cousins.
By that time, however, we of the Mother Country
have got our second wind, and so determined are we
to make the most of it that at last even the Editor
suddenly loses patience and says 'This correspondence must now cease.—Ed.' and wonders why on
earth he ever allowed anything so tedious and idiotic
to begin.

I pointed out to Laider one of the Australian letters
that had especially pleased me in the current issue.
It was from 'A Melbourne Man,' and was of the
abrupt kind which declares that 'all your correspon-
dents have been groping in the dark' and then settles
the whole matter in one short sharp flash. The flash
in this instance was 'Reason is faith, faith reason—
that is all we know on earth and all we need to
know.' The writer then inclosed his card and was,
etc., 'A Melbourne Man.' I said to Laider how very

restful it was, after influenza, to read anything that meant nothing whatsoever. Laider was inclined to take the letter more seriously than I, and to be mildly metaphysical. I said that for me faith and reason were two separate things, and (as I am no good at metaphysics, however mild) I offered a definite example, to coax the talk on to ground where I should· be safe. 'Palmistry, for example,' I said. 'Deep down in my heart I believe in palmistry.'

Laider turned in his chair. 'You believe in palmistry?'

I hesitated. 'Yes, somehow I do. Why? I haven't the slightest notion. I can give myself all sorts of reasons for laughing it to scorn. My common sense utterly rejects it. Of course the shape of the hand means something—is more or less an index of character. But the idea that my past and future are neatly mapped out on my palms——' I shrugged my shoulders.

'You don't like that idea?' asked Laider in his gentle, rather academic voice.

'I only say it's a grotesque idea.'

'Yet you do believe in it?'

'I've a grotesque belief in it, yes.'

'Are you sure your reason for calling this idea "grotesque" isn't merely that you dislike it?'

'Well,' I said, with the thrilling hope that he was a companion in absurdity, 'doesn't it seem grotesque to *you*?'

'It seems strange.'

'You believe in it?'

'Oh, absolutely.'

'Hurrah!'

He smiled at my pleasure, and I, at the risk of re-entanglement in metaphysics, claimed him as standing shoulder to shoulder with me against 'A Melbourne Man.' This claim he gently disputed. 'You may think me very prosaic,' he said, 'but I can't believe without evidence.'

'Well, I'm equally prosaic and equally at a disadvantage: I can't take my own belief as evidence, and I've no other evidence to go on.'

He asked me if I had ever made a study of palmistry. I said I had read one of Desbarolles' books years ago, and one of Heron-Allen's. But, he asked, had I tried to test them by the lines on my own hands or on the hands of my friends? I confessed that my actual practice in palmistry had been of a merely passive kind—the prompt extension of my palm to any one who would be so good as to 'read' it and truckle for a few minutes to my egoism. (I hoped Laider might do this.)

'Then, I almost wonder,' he said, with his sad smile, 'that you haven't lost your belief, after all the nonsense you must have heard. There are so many young girls who go in for palmistry. I am sure all the five foolish virgins were "awfully keen on it" and used to say "You can be led, but not driven," and "You are likely to have a serious illness between the ages of forty and forty-five," and "You are by nature rather lazy, but can be very energetic by fits and starts." And most of the professionals, I'm told, are as silly as the young girls.'

For the honour of the profession, I named three

practitioners whom I had found really good at reading character. He asked whether any of them had been right about past events. I confessed that, as a matter of fact, all three of them had been right in the main. This seemed to amuse him. He asked whether any of them had predicted anything which had since come true. I confessed that all three had predicted that I should do several things which I had since done rather unexpectedly. He asked if I didn't accept this as at any rate a scrap of evidence. I said I could only regard it as a fluke—a rather remarkable fluke.

The superiority of his sad smile was beginning to get on my nerves. I wanted him to see that he was as absurd as I. 'Suppose,' I said, 'suppose for sake of argument that you and I are nothing but helpless automata created to do just this and that, and to have just that and this done to us. Suppose in fact, we *haven't* any free will whatsoever. Is it likely or conceivable that the Power that fashioned us would take the trouble to jot down in cipher on our hands just what was in store for us?'

Laider did not answer this question, he did but annoyingly ask me another. 'You believe in free will?'

'Yes, of course. I'll be hanged if I'm an automaton.'

'And you believe in free will just as in palmistry—without any reason?'

'Oh no. Everything points to our having free will.'

'Everything? What, for instance?'

This rather cornered me. I dodged out, as lightly as I could, by saying 'I suppose *you* would say it was written in my hand that I should be a believer in free will.'

'Ah, I've no doubt it is.'

I held out my palms. But, to my great disappointment, he looked quickly away from them. He had ceased to smile. There was agitation in his voice as he explained that he never looked at people's hands now. 'Never now—never again.' He shook his head as though to beat off some memory.

I was much embarrassed by my indiscretion. I hastened to tide over the awkward moment by saying that if *I* could read hands I wouldn't, for fear of the awful things I might see there.

'Awful things, yes,' he whispered, nodding at the fire.

'Not,' I said in self-defence, 'that there's anything very awful, so far as I know, to be read in *my* hands.'

He turned his gaze from the fire to me. 'You aren't a murderer, for example?'

'Oh, no,' I replied, with a nervous laugh.

'*I* am.'

This was a more than awkward, it was a painful, moment for me; and I am afraid I must have started or winced, for he instantly begged my pardon. 'I don't know,' he exclaimed, 'why I said it. I'm usually a very reticent man. But sometimes—' He pressed his brow. 'What you must think of me!'

I begged him to dismiss the matter from his mind.

'It's very good of you to say that; but—I've placed myself as well as you in a false position. I ask you to believe that I'm not the sort of man who is "wanted" or ever was "wanted" by the police. I should be bowed out of any police-station at which I gave myself up. I'm not a murderer in any bald sense of the word. No.'

My face must have perceptibly brightened, for 'Ah,' he said, 'don't imagine I'm not a murderer at all. Morally, I am.' He looked at the clock. I pointed out that the night was young. He assured me that his story was not a long one. I assured him that I hoped it was. He said I was very kind. I denied this. He warned me that what he had to tell might rather tend to stiffen my unwilling faith in palmistry, and to shake my opposite and cherished faith in free will. I said 'Never mind.' He stretched his hands pensively toward the fire. I settled myself back in my chair.

'My hands,' he said, staring at the backs of them, 'are the hands of a very weak man. I dare say you know enough of palmistry to see that for yourself. You notice the slightness of the thumbs and of the two "little" fingers. They are the hands of a weak and over-sensitive man—a man without confidence, a man who would certainly waver in an emergency. Rather Hamlet-ish hands,' he mused. 'And I'm like Hamlet in other respects, too: I'm no fool, and I've rather a noble disposition, and I'm unlucky. But Hamlet was luckier than I in one thing: he was a murderer by accident, whereas the murders that I committed one day fourteen years ago—for I must tell you it wasn't one murder, but many murders that I committed—were all of them due to the wretched inherent weakness of my own wretched self.

'I was twenty-six—no, twenty-seven years old, and rather a nondescript person, as I am now. I was supposed to have been called to the Bar. In fact, I believe I *had* been called to the Bar. I hadn't listened to the call. I never intended to practise, and I never did practise. I only wanted an excuse in the eyes of the world for existing. I suppose the nearest I have ever come to practising is now at this moment: I am defending a murderer. My father had left me well enough provided with money. I was able to go my own desultory way, riding my hobbies where I would. I had a good stableful of hobbies. Palmistry was one of them. I was rather ashamed of this one. It seemed to me absurd, as it seems to you. Like you, though, I believed in it. Unlike you, I had done more than merely read a book or so about it. I had read innumerable books about it. I had taken casts of all my friends' hands. I had tested and tested again the points at which Desbarolles dissented from the gipsies, and—well, enough that I had gone into it all rather thoroughly, and was as sound a palmist as a man may be without giving his whole life to palmistry.

'One of the first things I had seen in my own hand, as soon as I had learned to read it, was that at about the age of twenty-six I should have a narrow escape from death—from a violent death. There was a clean break in the life-line, and a square joining it—the protective square, you know. The markings were precisely the same in both hands. It was to be the narrowest escape possible. And I wasn't going to escape without injury, either. That is what bothered me. There was a faint line connecting the break in the life-line with a star on the line of health. Against that star was another square. I was to recover from

the injury, whatever it might be. Still, I didn't
exactly look forward to it. Soon after I had reached
the age of twenty-five, I began to feel uncomfortable.
The thing might be going to happen at any moment.
In palmistry, you know, it is impossible to pin an
event down hard and fast to one year. This particular
event was to be when I was *about* twenty-six; it
mightn't be till I was twenty-seven; it might be while
I was only twenty-five.

'And I used to tell myself that it mightn't be at all.
My reason rebelled against the whole notion of
palmistry, just as yours does. I despised my faith in
the thing, just as you despise yours. I used to try
not to be so ridiculously careful as I was whenever
I crossed a street. I lived in London at that time.
Motor-cars had not yet come in, but—what hours, all
told, I must have spent standing on curbs, very
circumspect, very lamentable! It was a pity, I suppose, that I had no definite occupation—something
to take me out of myself. I was one of the victims of
private means. There came a time when I drove in
four-wheelers rather than in hansoms, and was
doubtful of four-wheelers. Oh, I assure you, I was
very lamentable indeed.

'If a railway-journey could be avoided, I avoided
it. My uncle had a place in Hampshire. I was very
fond of him and of his wife. Theirs was the only
house I ever went to stay in now. I was there for a
week in November, not long after my twenty-seventh
birthday. There were other people staying there, and
at the end of the week we all travelled back to London
together. There were six of us in the carriage:

Colonel Elbourn and his wife, and their daughter, a girl of seventeen; and another married couple, the Blakes. I had been at Winchester with Blake, but had hardly seen him since that time. He was in the Indian Civil, and was home on leave. He was sailing for India next week. His wife was to remain in England for some months, and then join him out there. They had been married five years. She was now just twenty-four years old. He told me that this was her age.

'The Elbourns I had never met before. They were charming people. We had all been very happy together. The only trouble had been that on the last night, at dinner, my uncle asked me if I still went in for "the gipsy business," as he always called it; and of course the three ladies were immensely excited, and implored me to "do" their hands. I told them it was all nonsense, I said I had forgotten all I once knew, I made various excuses; and the matter dropped. It was quite true that I had given up reading hands. I avoided anything that might remind me of what was in my own hands. And so, next morning, it was a great bore to me when, soon after the train started, Mrs. Elbourn said it would be "too cruel" of me if I refused to do their hands now. Her daughter and Mrs. Blake also said it would be "brutal"; and they were all taking off their gloves, and—well, of course I had to give in.

'I went to work methodically on Mrs. Elbourn's hands, in the usual way, you know, first sketching the character from the backs of them; and there was the usual hush, broken by the usual little noises—grunts of assent from the husband, cooings of recognition from the daughter. Presently I asked to see the palms, and from them I filled in the details of Mrs. Elbourn's character before going on to the events in her life. But while I talked I was calculating how old Mrs. Elbourn might be. In my first glance at her palms I had seen that she could not have been less than twenty-five when she married. The daughter was seventeen. Suppose the daughter had been born a year later—how old would the mother be? Forty-three, yes. Not less than that, poor woman!'

Laider looked at me. 'Why "poor woman," you wonder? Well, in that first glance I had seen other things than her marriage-line. I had seen a very complete break in the lines of life and of fate. I had seen violent death there. At what age? Not later, not possibly *later*, than forty-three. While I talked to her about the things that had happened in her girlhood, the back of my brain was hard at work on those marks of catastrophe. I was horribly wondering that she was still alive. It was impossible that between her and that catastrophe there could be more than a few short months. And all the time I was talking; and I suppose I acquitted myself well, for I remember that when I ceased I had a sort of ovation from the Elbourns.

'It was a relief to turn to another pair of hands. Mrs. Blake was an amusing young creature, and her hands were very characteristic, and prettily odd in form. I allowed myself to be rather whimsical about her nature, and, having begun in that vein, I went on in it—somehow—even after she had turned her palms. In those palms were reduplicated the signs

I had seen in Mrs. Elbourn's. It was as though they had been copied neatly out. The only difference was in the placing of them; and it was this difference that was the most horrible point. The fatal age in Mrs. Blake's hands was—not past, no, for here *she* was. But she might have died when she was twenty-one. Twenty-three seemed to be the utmost span. She was twenty-four, you know.

'I have said that I am a weak man. And you will have good proof of that directly. Yet I showed a certain amount of strength that day—yes, even on that day which has humiliated and saddened the rest of my life. Neither my face nor my voice betrayed me when in the palms of Dorothy Elbourn I was again confronted with those same signs. She was all for knowing the future, poor child! I believe I told her all manner of things that were to be. And she had no future—none, none in *this* world—except——

'And then, while I talked, there came to me suddenly a suspicion. I wondered it hadn't come before. You guess what it was? It made me feel very cold and strange. I went on talking. But, also, I went on—quite separately—thinking. The suspicion wasn't a certainty. This mother and daughter were always together. What was to befall the one might anywhere—anywhere—befall the other. But a like fate, in an equally near future, was in store for that other lady. The coincidence was curious, very. Here we all were together—here; they and I—I who was narrowly to escape, so soon now, what they, so soon now, were to suffer. Oh, there was an inference to be drawn. Not a *sure* inference, I told myself. And always

I was talking, talking, and the train was swinging and swaying noisily along—to what? It was a fast train. Our carriage was near the engine. I was talking loudly. Full well I had known what I should see in the Colonel's hands. I told myself I had not known. I told myself that even now the thing I dreaded was not sure to be. Don't think I was dreading it for myself. I wasn't so "lamentable" as all that—now. It was only of them that I thought—only for them. I hurried over the Colonel's character and career; I was perfunctory. It was Blake's hands that I wanted. *They* were the hands that mattered. If *they* had the marks—— Remember, Blake was to start for India in the coming week, his wife was to remain in England. They would be apart. Therefore——

'And the marks were there. And I did nothing— nothing but hold forth on the subtleties of Blake's character. There was a thing for me to do. I wanted to do it. I wanted to spring to the window and pull the communication-cord. Quite a simple thing to do. Nothing easier than to stop a train. You just give a sharp pull, and the train slows down, comes to a stand-still. And the Guard appears at your window. You explain to the Guard.

'Nothing easier than to tell him there is going to be a collision. Nothing easier than to insist that you and your friends and every other passenger in the train must get out at once. . . . There *are* easier things than this? Things that need less courage than this? Some of *them* I could have done, I daresay. This thing I was going to do. Oh, I was determined that I would do it—directly.

'I had said all I had to say about Blake's hands. I had brought my entertainment to an end. I had been thanked and complimented all round. I was quite at liberty. I was going to do what I had to do. I was determined, yes.

'We were near the outskirts of London. The air was grey, thickening; and Dorothy Elbourn had said, "Oh, this horrible old London! I suppose there's the same old fog!" And presently I heard her father saying something about "prevention" and "a short act of Parliament" and "anthracite." And I sat and listened and agreed and——'

Laider closed his eyes. He passed his hand slowly through the air.

'I had a racking headache. And when I said so, I was told not to talk. I was in bed, and the nurses were always telling me not to talk. I was in a hospital. I knew that. But I didn't know why I was there. One day I thought I should like to know why, and so I asked. I was feeling much better now. They told me, by degrees, that I had had concussion of the brain. I had been brought there unconscious, and had remained unconscious for forty-eight hours. I had been in an accident—a railway accident. This seemed to me odd. I had arrived quite safely at my uncle's place, and I had no memory of any journey since that. In cases of concussion, you know, it's not uncommon for the patient to forget all that happened just before the accident; there may be a blank of several hours. So it was in my case. One day my uncle was allowed to come and see me. And somehow, suddenly, at sight of him, the blank was filled in. I remembered, in a flash, everything. I was quite calm, though. Or I made myself seem so, for I wanted to know how the collision had happened. My uncle told me that the engine-driver had failed to see a signal because of the fog, and our train had crashed into a goods-train. I didn't ask him about the people who were with me. You see, there was no need to ask. Very gently my uncle began to tell me, but—I had begun to talk strangely, I suppose. I remember the fright-ened look of my uncle's face, and the nurse scolding him in whispers.

'After that, all a blur. It seems that I became very ill indeed, wasn't expected to live.

'However, I live.'

There was a long silence. Laider did not look at me, nor I at him. The fire was burning low, and he watched it.

At length he spoke. 'You despise me. Naturally. I despise myself.'

'No, I don't despise you; but——'

'You blame me.' I did not meet his gaze. 'You blame me,' he repeated.

'Yes.'

'And there, if I may say so, you are a little unjust. It isn't my fault that I was born weak.'

'But a man may conquer weakness.'

'Yes, if he is endowed with the strength for that.'

His fatalism drew from me a gesture of disgust. 'Do you really mean,' I asked, 'that because you didn't pull that cord, you *couldn't* have pulled it?'

'Yes.'

'And it's written in your hands that you couldn't?'

He looked at the palms of his hands. 'They are the hands of a very weak man,' he said.

'A man so weak that he cannot believe in the possibility of free will for himself or for any one?'

'They are the hands of an intelligent man, who can weigh evidence and see things as they are.'

'But answer me: Was it fore-ordained that you should not pull that cord?'

'It was fore-ordained.'

'And was it actually marked in your hands that you were not going to pull it?'

'Ah, well, you see, it's rather the things one *is* going to do that are actually marked. The things one *isn't* going to do,—the innumerable negative things, —how could one expect *them* to be marked?'

'But the consequences of what one leaves undone may be positive?'

'Horribly positive,' he winced. 'My hand is the hand of a man who has suffered a great deal in later life.'

'And was it the hand of a man *destined* to suffer?'

'Oh, yes. I thought I told you that.'

There was a pause.

'Well,' I said, with awkward sympathy, 'I suppose all hands are the hands of people destined to suffer.'

'Not of people destined to suffer so much as *I* have suffered—as I still suffer.'

The insistence of his self-pity chilled me, and I harked back to a question he had not straightly answered. 'Tell me: Was it marked in your hands that you were not going to pull that cord?'

Again he looked at his hands, and then, having

pressed them for a moment to his face, 'It was marked very clearly,' he answered, 'in *their* hands.'

Two or three days after this colloquy there had occurred to me in London an idea—an ingenious and comfortable doubt. How was Laider to be sure that his brain, recovering from concussion, had *remembered* what happened in the course of that railway-journey? How was he to know that his brain hadn't simply, in its abeyance, *invented* all this for him? It might be that he had never seen those signs in those hands. Assuredly, here was a bright loop-hole. I had forthwith written to Laider, pointing it out.

This was the letter which now, at my second visit, I had found miserably pent on the letter-board. I remembered my promise to rescue it. I arose from the retaining fireside, stretched my arms, yawned, and went forth to fulfil my Christian purpose. There was no one in the hall. The 'shower' had at length ceased. The sun had positively come out, and the front door had been thrown open in its honour. Everything along the sea-front was beautifully gleaming, drying, shimmering. But I was not to be diverted from my errand. I went to the letter-board. And—my letter was not there! Resourceful and plucky little thing—it had escaped! I did hope it would not be captured and brought back. Perhaps the alarm had already been raised by the tolling of that great bell which warns the inhabitants for miles around that a letter has broken loose from the letter-board. I had a vision of my envelope skimming wildly along the coast-line, pursued by the old but active waiter and a breathless pack of local worthies. I saw it out-distancing them all, dodging past coast-guards, doubling on its tracks, leaping breakwaters, un-luckily injuring itself, losing speed, and at last, in a splendour of desperation, taking to the open sea. But suddenly I had another idea. Perhaps Laider had returned?

He had. I espied afar on the sands a form that was recognisably, by the listless droop of it, his. I was glad and sorry—rather glad, because he completed the scene of last year; and very sorry because this time we should be at each other's mercy: no restful silence and liberty, for either of us, this time. Perhaps he had been told I was here, and had gone out to avoid me while he yet could. Oh weak, weak! Why palter? I put on my hat and coat, and marched out to meet him.

'Influenza, of course?' we asked simultaneously.

There is a limit to the time which one man may spend in talking to another about his own influenza; and presently, as we paced the sands, I felt that Laider had passed this limit. I wondered that he didn't break off and thank me now for my letter. He must have read it. He ought to have thanked me for it at once. It was a very good letter, a remarkable letter. But surely he wasn't waiting to answer it by post? His silence about it gave me the absurd sense of having taken a liberty, confound him! He was evidently ill at ease while he talked. But it wasn't for me to help him out of his difficulty, whatever that might be. It was for him to remove the strain imposed on myself.

Abruptly, after a long pause, he did now manage to say, 'It was—very good of you to—to write me that letter.' He told me he had only just got it, and he drifted away into otiose explanations of this fact. I thought he might at least say it was a remarkable letter; and you can imagine my annoyance when he said, after another interval, 'I was very much touched indeed.' I had wished to be convincing, not touching. I can't bear to be called touching.

'Don't you,' I asked, 'think it *is* quite possible that your brain invented all those memories of what— what happened before that accident?'

He drew a sharp sigh. 'You make me feel very guilty.'

'That's exactly what I tried to make you *not* feel!'

'I know, yes. That's why I feel so guilty.'

We had paused in our walk. He stood nervously prodding the hard wet sand with his walking-stick. 'In a way,' he said, 'your theory was quite right. But— it didn't go far enough. It's not only possible, it's a fact, that I didn't see those signs in those hands. I never examined those hands. They weren't there. *I* wasn't there. I haven't an uncle in Hampshire, even. I never had.'

I, too, prodded the sand. 'Well,' I said at length, 'I do feel rather a fool.'

'I've no right even to beg your pardon, but—'

'Oh, I'm not vexed. Only—I rather wish you hadn't told me this.'

'I wish I hadn't had to. It was your kindness, you see, that forced me. By trying to take an imaginary load off my conscience, you laid a very real one on it.'

'I'm sorry. But you, of your own free will, you know, exposed your conscience to me last year. I don't yet quite understand why you did that.'

'No, of course not. I don't deserve that you should. But I think you will. May I explain? I'm afraid I've talked a great deal already about my influenza, and I shan't be able to keep it out of my explanation. Well, my weakest point—I told you this last year, but it happens to be perfectly true that my weakest point —is my will. Influenza, as you know, fastens unerringly on one's weakest point. It doesn't attempt to undermine my imagination. That would be a forlorn hope. I have, alas! a very strong imagination. At ordinary times my imagination allows itself to be governed by my will. My will keeps it in check by constant nagging. But when my will isn't strong enough even to nag, then my imagination stampedes. I become even as a little child. I tell myself the most preposterous fables, and—the trouble is—I can't help telling them to my friends. Until I've thoroughly shaken off influenza, I'm not fit company for any one. I perfectly realise this, and I have the good sense to go right away till I'm quite well again. I come here usually. It seems absurd, but I must confess I was sorry last year when we fell into conversation. I knew I should very soon be letting myself go, or rather, very soon be swept away. Perhaps I ought to have warned you; but—I'm a rather shy man. And then you mentioned the subject of palmistry. You said you believed in it. I wondered at that. I had once read Desbarolles' book about it, but I am bound to say I thought the whole thing very great nonsense indeed.'

'Then,' I gasped, 'it isn't even true that you believe in palmistry?'

'Oh, no. But I wasn't able to tell you that. You had begun by saying that you believed in palmistry, and then you proceeded to scoff at it. While you scoffed I saw myself as a man with a terribly good reason for *not* scoffing; and in a flash I saw the terribly good reason; I had the whole story—at least I had the broad outlines of it—clear before me.'

'You hadn't ever thought of it before?' He shook his head. My eyes beamed. 'The whole thing was a sheer improvisation?'

'Yes,' said Laider, humbly, 'I am as bad as all that. I don't say that all the details of the story I told you that evening were filled in at the very instant of its conception. I was filling them in while we talked about palmistry in general, and while I was waiting for the moment when my story would come in most effectively. And I've no doubt I added some extra touches in the course of the actual telling. Don't imagine that I took the slightest pleasure in deceiving you. It's only my will, not my conscience, that is weakened after influenza. I simply can't help telling what I've made up, and telling it to the best of my ability. But I'm thoroughly ashamed all the time.'

'Not of your ability, surely?'

'Yes, of that, too,' he said with his sad smile. 'I always feel that I'm not doing justice to my idea.'

'You are too stern a critic, believe me.'

'It is very kind of you to say that. You are very kind altogether. Had I known that you were so essentially a man of the world—in the best sense of that term—I shouldn't have so much dreaded seeing you just now and having to confess to you. But I'm not going to take advantage of your urbanity and your easy-going ways. I hope that some day we may meet somewhere when I haven't had influenza and am a not wholly undesirable acquaintance. As it is, I refuse to let you associate with me. I am an older man than you, and so I may without impertinence warn you against having anything to do with me.'

I deprecated this advice, of course; but for a man of weakened will, he showed great firmness. 'You,' he said, 'in your heart of hearts, don't want to have to walk and talk continually with a person who might at any moment try to bamboozle you with some ridiculous tale. And I, for my part, don't want to degrade myself by trying to bamboozle any one— especially one whom I have taught to see through me. Let the two talks we have had be as though they had not been. Let us bow to each other, as last year, but let that be all. Let us follow in all things the precedent of last year.'

With a smile that was almost gay he turned on his heel, and moved away with a step that was almost brisk. I was a little disconcerted. But I was also more than a little glad. The restfulness of silence, the charm of liberty—these things were not, after all, forfeit. My heart thanked Laider for that; and throughout the week I loyally seconded him in the system he had laid down for us. All was as it had been last year. We did not smile to each other, we merely bowed, when we entered or left the dining-room or smoking-room, and when we met on the widespread sands or in that shop which had a small and faded, but circulating, library.

Once or twice in the course of the week it did occur to me that perhaps Laider had told the simple truth at our first interview and an ingenious lie at our second. I frowned at this possibility. The idea of any one wishing to be quit of *me* was most distasteful. However, I was to find reassurance. On the last evening of my stay, I suggested, in the small smoking-room, that he and I should, as sticklers for precedent, converse. We did so, very pleasantly. And after a while I happened to say that I had seen this afternoon a great number of sea-gulls flying close to the shore.

'Sea-gulls?' said Laider, turning in his chair.

'Yes. And I don't think I had ever realised how extraordinarily beautiful they are when their wings catch the light.'

'Beautiful?' Laider threw a quick glance at me and away from me. 'You think them beautiful?'

'Surely.'

'Well, perhaps they are, yes; I suppose they are. But—I don't like seeing them. They always remind me of something—rather an awful thing—that once happened to me.' . . .

It was a very awful thing indeed.

FELIX ARGALLO AND
WALTER LEDGETT

FELIX ARGALLO AND
WALTER LEDGETT

March 19th, 1927

I MARK yesterday with a white stone. I made £900 yesterday.

Of this exploit I am all the gladder to write because it was not a mere vulgar fluke of the race-course or the stock-market, such as might befall me were I rich. It was the decent result of a wise step that I took quietly fifteen years ago. And that step would never have been taken had I not previously, in sheer kindness of heart, done a deed for which, when I shall have told you of it, you will praise me. And yet another reason for me to unfold my tale is that I shall thereby link my name with two names that are very illustrious—those of Felix Argallo and Walter Ledgett.

It may be that in these days, among the young, Argallo's name is the main thing about him. His books are but little read, I daresay, save by us elders. Argallo was primarily a man of feeling: his whole philosophy was founded on his emotions; and I am told that emotions are now not held in high esteem by the young. To take things as they come, and to examine them rather carefully, and to dismiss them rather lightly, appears to be the present fashion. Such things as pity and love and joy and indignation

are incorrect. Joy was a thing alien to Argallo's
nature, certainly; but of what avail would this point
in his favour be as against his genius for pity? Pity,
profound and austerely tender pity, was the keynote
of all his writings. He could not, as has often been
pointed out, write of anything that did not sadden
him. This would have been a serious limitation to his
genius, but for the fact that so few things in this world
did *not* sadden him. Sometimes it was not quite easy
to understand what he was pitying—what maiden in
distress the old knight-errant was eager to rescue,
and just what her distress was. His style was difficult.
But it was not the less magnificent. Those long-
drawn cadences of his, those never-faltering sonor-
ousnesses, which were the voice of his soul, are surely
among the highest achievements in English prose;
and it is doubtful whether any man of purely English
blood could have given them to us; beside them
Ruskin's style seems tame, halting. But eloquence,
with what it springs from, is out of date. It may come
in again? Well, then Argallo will come in again,
amidst the plaudits of the young.

His first entry had made no stir at all. Few people
had been aware of it. Many years passed before his
presence was noticed by others than those few. In
1894, when I came down from Oxford, I had never
heard his name; and it was only because his name
looked rather promising, somehow, that I one day
paid threepence to the keeper of a second-hand
bookshop in Praed Street and bore away with me a
copy of 'The Wall of Aloes.' The book was twelve
years old, its cover was very dingy, its pages were

mostly uncut; and as I cast my eye over some of
the pages that were open to inspection I felt that the
author's name had raised false hopes. But, unlike the
critics of that period and of the foregoing period, I
persevered; and soon I was enthralled. I do not say
that a new star had swum into my ken. That would
strike too cheery a note. Rather had I roamed into
a dim twilight where great and noble things were
faintly discernible, looming suddenly out upon me,
and giving place to others before I had gauged their
import. Next day, when I had finished the book,
I was already a keen enough Argalloist to read it all
over again. With clearer understanding came a higher
enthusiasm, on the wings of which I sped around to
many bookshops in quest of other works by the
unknown god. I would not believe that there were
no others; but my incredulity was not confirmed by
any of my friends, and I might have begun to waver
had I not—suddenly, blessedly—happened upon
'A Bare Bodkin.'

This work was at that time aged only five years,
and thus gave me a sense of comparative nearness
to its creator; but it gave me also a sense of remote-
ness from him: I doubted whether he were still
alive. The idea of suicide had often commended
itself to the weak and flaccid—to just the kind of
people who would not carry it out. But Argallo, as
I had discerned through 'The Wall of Aloes' had at
some time been a man of action, a fighter. Had he
since been fighting his own theories? Or had he
strengthened them with his own death? I tried to
believe that he would in his austerity withhold

from himself the pity that he lavished on his fellow-beings, and would go stoically on to the natural end. But I was as surprised as I was glad to hear, a month or so after my purchase of 'A Bare Bodkin,' that he was still with us.

'With us' is perhaps not quite the phrase to use about a man living at Penge; and Penge was the scene of the great survival. Professor James Fitzmaurice Kelly, whom I met now for the first time, was my informant. I gathered that he (great gun that he was in Anglo-Hispanic scholarship) had helped Argallo by getting him commissions to translate Spanish works. I gathered also that Argallo had been born and bred in England, son of an Englishwoman and of a Spanish refugee who had fought in the first Carlist War. He himself, filially Carlist in his early manhood, had gone out to Spain and fought, with much gallantry and many wounds, throughout the insurrections of 1872–1876, afterwards returning to England and trying, with scant success, to live by his pen. He had at some time married an Englishwoman, but was now a widower, and rather a recluse. The Professor highly praised Argallo as translator, and seemed glad that I liked—glad that any one should like—Argallo's own books. Of these, he said, there must be quite half-a-dozen. He had them and would lend me them. He lent me them, and soon my fervour was such that he asked me to meet Argallo himself at luncheon. 'You must be prepared for a queer sad old fellow,' he said; but I needed no such warning.

Face to face with Argallo, I wondered only that

he fitted so exactly my preconception of him. The long, gaunt, concave figure; the great melancholy dark eyes deep-set beneath a brow so wide that it seemed disproportionate even on so tall a man; the great aquiline nose; the small lips compressed into a short tight line by the soul's need to govern its sensibility; the sallowness, the shawnness, the close-cropped iron-grey hair; the shabbiness, but scrupulous neatness, of the clothes; the dignity, coupled with the painful shyness of the demeanour—all these things and all else about Mr. Argallo were as I had expected and had wished. He had not been told that a third person was to be present; otherwise, said the Professor, he might not have come. I effaced myself as much as possible, so that the stormer of Castilian barricades should not be frightened. I hoped he would presently like me. That he already pitied me as much as he feared me was a matter of course; but I wanted to be liked too. And so well did I strive towards that goal that Mr. Argallo actually said, when he took leave of us, that if ever I found myself in his neighbourhood he would be very glad to see me.

Most of my elder readers, doubtless, visited that little house in Penge as soon as it was acquired for the nation. Ermyntrude Road, they will agree, is a deadly thoroughfare. It was just as deadly in the 'nineties. Nor was Argallo's home brighter than it is to-day. It was the saddest of settings for the saddest of hidalgos. And the measure of my fervour is that I did, in the course of years, go to it frequently, and loved going.

I never asked leave to bring anybody with me. Others there soon were who would have liked to come, for my fervour had soon infected many of my friends—all of them, indeed, who had spiritual insight and a scent for fine literature. But Moses, that egoist, had gone alone up Mount Sinai, and always alone went I down to Penge, there to breathe, between the hours of four and six—four, the hour when Argallo ceased work, and six, the hour when he ate something—an atmosphere heavily-laden with Castilian courtesy and gloom and genius. I never told him that I constantly referred to him and to his works in articles for the weekly press; nor did I let him know that some of my friends were doing so. His pride would have been wounded to the quick by any inkling of any such aid. He earned enough by his translations to keep body and soul together; and his desire that his present and future work should be published in book-form was balanced by that power for pity which was so great as to exclude not even publishers from its scope. When the great change in his life came I never hinted to him that I and my friends and *their* friends—the ever-growing band of us perceivers—were in any sort responsible for it.

And indeed this change, which occurred in the Spring of 1905, immediately after the publication of 'Last Shadows' was so abrupt and complete a peripety that we ourselves were too dazed to take full credit for it. We poor sappers and miners were blinded, were deafened, by the vast explosion. It seemed less like a work of our own than like some awful phenomenon of brute Nature. We had never supposed that Argallo was the one and only great writer the world had yet possessed. But the Press, for the most part, held that opinion.

Walter Ledgett, I remember, was in frank agreement with the Press. It would have been strange if so generous, so swiftly impressionable a creature had felt any doubts in the matter. In the earlier years of my acquaintance with him, he too had been a reviewer of books, and had seldom written a review without heartfelt conviction that the occasion was unique. Deeply as he revered the established names in literature, he was wildly susceptible to almost anybody's 'latest.' He was a true book-lover. I had not, however, at any time, breathed to him the name of Argallo. I had felt that he would not be of service to the cause. Only about his own books did his judgment seem to me sound. 'My stuff' he called them; and his modesty, like everything else about him (except, as I thought, his talent), was perfectly genuine. He was the most unpretentious of dear little men. At the Savage Club and the Authors', at the Playgoers and the Yorick, there was no man more popular than 'Walt;' and he seemed to be always at all four of them, bustling around, buttonholing, radiating innocence from his fresh round face. He was the brightest of untiring little busybodies— always joyously organising a dinner in honour of somebody, or a subscription for somebody's widow, or an illuminated address to some great man. In the year of Argallo's apocalypse he was nearing the age

of forty, and was making a great deal of money by
his work; but his eye was as guileless, and his hair as
curly, and his bearing as undistinguished as ever. He
had dramatised his last year's novel, 'Sweet Lady
Caprice;' and this was being played with great success at the Strand Theatre. His cape-and-sword
drama, 'A Berserker in the Bastille,' had been produced elsewhere a year or so before, with equal
success, and in the subsequent form of a novel was
widely read by adults of the infantile persuasion.
These plays of his, with two or three others that had
held the boards, created a demand for even the things
he did as a labour of love—the dear offspring of his
veneration for mighty names and of his annual walking tour in the month of August. 'Wordsworth's
Windermere,' 'In Stevenson's Cevennes,' 'A Tramp
Through Hardy-Land,' 'Where Shelley Roamed'—
and all the rest of them—became very marketable
indeed. But their author was quite unspoilt. Nor
indeed did his clubmates try to spoil him. He was, as
ever, the victim of many hoaxes. Anybody with a
solemn face could tell him the most preposterous
things and be believed. Frank chaff, on the other
hand, was understood by him quite well and taken
with delight. Whenever he was in the chair at a house-
dinner, some one would be sure to shout along the
table, 'Hullo, Walt! What are *you* doing there?' and
'My dear chap, ask me another!' he would beam-
ingly shout back.

It is true that in the photographs that were taken
of him for the illustrated papers there was a touch
of solemnity, of cerebration. Either the brow would

be propped up by the right hand and partly covered
by it, or the left hand would be clutching and wholly
covering the chin. One day when I was lunching at
the Savage, as guest of my friend Mostyn Pigott,
Ledgett joined us at table; and my host insisted to
him that those pensive attitudes towards the camera
were obvious precautions.—'At Elliott and Fry's,
Walt, you feel that your forehead is unimpressive:
you daren't show it. At Russell's you remember your
weak chin: you hastily hide it. Quite right too! But
not thorough enough! Next time you go to Baker
Street, you must have one hand across your chin
and the other across your forehead. And by Jove,
I'll go with you, out of friendship, and stand behind
you, holding my hands across the middle part of your
face, old boy!' Ledgett almost rolled off his chair, in
spasms of delight at Mostyn's affectionate onslaught.
He simply could not take offence at anything a friend
said.

This disability was the more loveable because he
was not insensitive. So early as 1899 I had discovered
that outside the realms of good-fellowship he was
quite thin-skinned. Stevenson's Letters had recently
been published, and I had just begun to read them.
I met Ledgett in the Strand and asked if he had read
them yet. 'Yes—oh, yes—capital, aren't they?' This
was faint praise from Ledgett. Moreover, he blushed
as he spoke it, and parted from me rather abruptly.
I remembered these things when I came to a passage
in one of the later Samoan letters to R. A. M. ('Bob')
Stevenson:—'Dost knaw aught of a lad named Leget
or Legget? He writ me (but mon, I hae na keppit his

horrid screed) wanting to write a wee bookie anent me. He claimed to have met you. If you know him, do, like a good fellow, write to him—and tell him not to.' Poor little Ledgett! What a shame!

In the following Spring appeared the Life and Letters of Coventry Patmore, and I was very sorry to find there, at the close of an interesting letter to Mr. Wilfrid Meynell, 'Please say a sharp word to this Mr. L——. A man making his soul under the shadow of the Awful Gate doesn't want to be pestered to be the guest of a dining-club.' I made no reference to Patmore's epistolary charm when next I came across Ledgett, and was the more careful not to do so because I had heard that some friends of his at the Authors' Club had jovially greeted him as Mr. L—— and been stricken with remorse at sight of sudden moisture in his eyes. Not even by his cronies, from whom he could stand any amount of direct banter, could he bear to be rallied on an unkind snub.

When, a few years later, Bram Stoker's Life of Henry Irving was published, I was again very sorry. The biographer quoted, as 'an example both of the Chief's good judgment and of his diplomacy' the following note:—'Dear Stoker,—Have read W—— L——'s drama. Decidedly *not*, eh? Let the man down lightly. Greetings, H.I.'

This was less bad. There was a touch of kindness about it. But it was bad enough. And, though I am not of a nervous or suspicious habit, I began now to believe there was a conspiracy among the Fates that all Ledgett's failures to please great men should

ultimately be brought to light. I wished great men
would not die. I wished that if die they must their
letters should be destroyed. And when, in the Spring
of 1912, the Letters of George Meredith were given
to us, it was with a deep groan that I beheld these
words at the end of a letter written in 1889 to Leslie
Stephen:—'Yesterday an eager homunculus named
L—— struck foot across this threshold, sputter-
ing encomiastic cackle. He wanted me to be guest
of honour at some festal junket in town. Such
are the signs that England has heard of one's
existence. I salaam'd him off, but he was not an
easy goer.'

This was too much. I rose from my chair. Something must be done. I threw open the window and
leaned out into the night. This constant persecution
of Ledgett by the mighty dead must be put a stop to.
But how? I regretted that I was not a man of resource.
And in so doing (not that I would boast) I rather
underrated myself. For there came to me suddenly
an idea for a course of action. Nothing perhaps could
be done to deter the malign Fates. But the evil they
were bent on could be somewhat counteracted.
Having paced my room awhile, I sat down to my
writing-table.

And early in the afternoon of the next day I took
a cab to Wimbledon. Felix Argallo had now lived
there for six years, in an old house with a high-walled
garden. Penge had become impossible soon after the
apocalypse. Within a month of its publication in the
Spring, 'Last Shadows'—and with it all the previous

works—had come out in America too, of course.
America in such crises is less self-controlled than
England. There were strange doings. The principal
literary critic in Pittsburg lost his reason and had to
be placed under restraint; and the number of suicides
here and there was so large that in some of the States
the sale of 'A Bare Bodkin' was banned by the
authorities. And during the Summer months in
Ermyntrude Road the crowds of American tourists
standing outside Argallo's exposed refuge were too
great for his endurance. He had to live with the blinds
down; he could take exercise only after dark; his
health suffered. He didn't ever say he had heard that
I was the origin of all the new woes which had come
on him. But I think some ill-natured person must
have hinted as much to him; for his manner to me, in
that darkened sitting-room, was cold. Darkness and
confinement in a glare of bi-hemispheric publicity—
with the beginnings of hideously vast wealth thrown
in—were too much for Argallo's inveterate stoicism.
He began to pity *himself*.

Nor did the irruption of George Batford into his
life seem to comfort him. This youth, a nephew of
the late Mrs. Argallo, had been a clerk in some pro-
vincial firm of business, but had very unselfishly
thrown up his post in order to 'look after the old
gentleman.' He was a brisk, sensible young fellow;
and he 'handled' Argallo's 'rights' with great gusto,
and in a manner that wrung admiration from the
various publishers involved. It was he, too, that hit
on the house at Wimbledon and effected the purchase
of it and now 'ran' it very smoothly and well. It was

he that sent interviewers and photographers empty
away. 'Privacy is the biggest Ad,' he once said to me,
with a wink. He may have indiscreetly made this
remark to his uncle also. For Argallo seemed to be
oppressed even by the dignity of seclusion. His
health had been restored by his daily walks around
the garden. But his spirit had been well-nigh broken
by success. When he was not walking in the garden,
he was translating. The nephew obtained fabulous
offers even for these translations. The uncle shook
his head.

However, as I drove down to Wimbledon through
the Spring sunshine, I had little doubt that I could
persuade Argallo to grant me the MSS. that I needed.
I needed neither translations nor original work;
merely some to-be-dictated matter, for a purpose
which I thought would commend itself to him. True,
his self-pity had become a formidable rival to his
sorrow for mankind; but surely the special case that
I was going to lay before him would not leave him
unmoved, unhelpful? Nor was I disappointed. As we
paced the garden together (unbothered by prosaic
George, who was up in town on business) he was
moved, he was won; and presently, without a word,
he led me indoors to his study. There, with his grave
old courtesy, he placed a chair for me near to his
writing-table. I laid before him some sheets of note-
paper—several kinds of cheap note-paper—which I
had bought that morning. I sat down and sorted out
in my hands the MSS. that I had written overnight.
I cleared my throat. He dipped his pen in the ink and
wrote, at my dictation, as follows:—

43, Ermyntrude Road, Penge, S.E.
Monday, February 27th, 1898.

Dear Mr. Beerbohm,—I must unburden my
heart in thanks to you for bringing me acquainted with Walter Ledgett. He spent the
day here yesterday, and it was a day that will
be in my memory while life lasts. What a man!
I have known in my time many men of divers
races. But I swear on my conscience I have
never known one who—how shall I say it?—
gives more than your friend Ledgett. Others
may have his abundance. But they do not scatter
it, as he does. He arrived in a hansom in the
morning, I offered him what poor hospitality
I could, he did not leave before dusk. During
the afternoon, W. E. Henley—himself a fine
talker, as you know—came in to see me.

Argallo paused in his penmanship and looked at
me. 'W. E. Henley, the poet and critic?'

'Of course.'

'But I never knew him.'

'No? But what matter, Mr. Argallo? You never
knew Ledgett either.'

'True.'

And all the time Ledgett talked, talked, while
we listened, Henley and I, much as the fishes
listened to Arion's singing. You know my feeling about Ledgett's work. Well, the impression
that I had the other evening, when I met him
under your auspices, was right. The man is
greater than his work. *Credo quia incredibile.*

When Henley and I were alone, I said: 'How horrible that of all that he poured out to us nothing will remain!' And presently we had a sort of paper-game—Henley and I separately writing out all the best single phrases we could remember of his talk. Thank God, there is no jealousy in my nature. Ledgett makes a worm of me, but if I writhe it is only for joy. He promised he would come and see me again some day. I wonder if he will? How hideous an irony that such a man should be born into such a world as ours!

Thank you again.

Yours faithfully,
Felix Argallo.

P.S. L. spoke most kindly of you and of your work, which he thinks *extremely promising*—his own words, and he spoke them with great emphasis.

'End of first letter,' I said. 'Another sheet of paper now. That yellowish-greyish kind, perhaps' . . .

Clarke's Temperance Hotel,
    Walford Street,
        Tottenham Court Road.
        October 23rd, 1903.   Midnight.
Dear Max Beerbohm,—I came up to town this morning, for though I am, as you know, no playgoer and detest the English theatre, I never miss a Ledgett first night. What a play! Has he ever done anything so fine as that third act? I took my stand outside the Pit entrance early

in the afternoon, so as to be sure to have a place in the front row. It was a long wait, but really, such was my excitement, it passed almost in a flash. I think the gradual unfolding of the woman's character, as wrought on by the situation in the third act, is the finest *technical* feat Ledgett has yet achieved. Could you lunch with me here to-morrow? Table-d'hôte is at one o'clock. I want to talk of the play to some one who I know shares my feeling for Ledgett's work.

Yours sincerely,
Felix Argallo.

P.S. There was a man sitting next to me who did not applaud at the end of the first act, and I said something to him which I instantly regretted. Afterwards we became quite good friends. I could not help telling him that I knew Ledgett personally—that he had once come to my house. What weak vain creatures God's creatures are!

'End of letter. Thank you Mr. Argallo. Take another sheet, please. This one is from Penge again. You're sure I'm not tiring you?—no?'

43, Ermyntrude Road, Penge.
May 4th, 1904.

In strictest confidence.

My dear Max Beerbohm,—I came up to London yesterday to see my 'literary agent.' He had to give me the usual discouragement, poor man. But it is not about him that I am writing to you.

Leaving the Strand, I turned aimlessly westward and passed through Piccadilly (more than ever oppressed by the sadness of its gaiety). I then wandered into the Park. About halfway up the Drive (is that what it is called?) I, feeling tired, sat down on one of those green chairs, facing eastward. Presently a 'brougham' drew up at the break in the railings just opposite to me, and out of it stepped a tall young woman of extreme beauty. She gave some order to the coachman, who touched his hat, said 'Yes, your Excellency,' and drove away. What struck me even more than the beauty of her face was the expression of it—an extraordinary mingling, as it seemed to me, of hope and despair. She passed very quickly across the pathway to the grass beyond, nor had she gone far when I found myself following her, urged forward by the belief that I might somehow be of service to her. She made straight for a distant tree—an elm—under which were two chairs. I seated myself under another tree—a plane—some twenty yards away. She sat quite unconscious of any observer, straining her eyes in the direction whence she had come—always with that strange duality of expression. I was filled with an all the deeper compassion for her because, though evidently a married woman, she was hardly more than a girl in her teens, and also because, for all her high elegance and her air as of one accustomed to command, there was yet about her something that I can only describe as *servile*. Suddenly,

after 20 minutes or so of tense and rigid waiting, she sprang to her feet. A man was approaching from the distance. He came sauntering
along, twirling his stick round and round in the
air, with his hat tilted back from his forehead.
My first impression of his face, as he drew near,
was not pleasant. It seemed to me a cold and a
hard face. A moment later, repressing a cry, I
recognised the face of Walter Ledgett.

Argallo looked up from his task. 'Surely,' he said,
'this can only injure your friend.'

'Oh, not at all—quite the contrary. And of course
the name *Walter Ledgett* won't appear on the printed
page. When the time comes for your Letters to
appear, I shall ask the editor of them to omit *Walter
Ledgett* from this particular letter and to substitute
two strokes.'

'Then how is anybody to know whom you mean?'

'Whom *you* mean, Mr. Argallo. They'll know
whom you mean, or rather meant, by collating this
letter with your other letters to me. You never seemed
able to write to me about *anybody* but Ledgett. . . .
Shall we go on now?'

'Certainly, yes. Pardon me.' Argallo took up his pen.

I rose to my feet, stepped quickly behind my
plane tree—but not, I fear, before the new-
comer had seen and recognised me. I then
walked rapidly away, not once looking back.
I felt, as you may imagine, a great heaviness at
my heart. I had pitied the woman, but to her,
now, I gave hardly a thought'—

'I don't at all like that,' muttered my amanuensis.

'Why not? It shows the intensity of your feeling for Ledgett. Besides, the woman never existed— she's a figment, don't you see? Ledgett's a man of flesh and blood.'

'H'm. You're very glib. Well?'

—gave hardly a thought, except in so far as she might yet be a source of trouble to our friend. That wonderful white face was as full of strength as of beauty. It was the face of one who, cast off, might by some kind of persecution hinder our friend in his creative work. You yourself see much of Ledgett, and are in his confidence. Perhaps you know of this affair?—though, from hints you have let drop, I suppose it is only one of many. I should be glad if you could reassure me that there is nothing to fear for him and for his art.

Ever sincerely yours,
Felix Argallo.

'I sign my name to that with great reluctance,' growled the signatory.

'Well, then, let's have a postscript.'

P.S. I am less callous than I seem. That young face of anguish will haunt me always.

'Only one more, Mr. Argallo. This one may as well have a recent date—to show that you never faltered in the faith.'

Wimbledon.
December, 1911.

My dear Max,—

Argallo looked at me with sombre irony. 'Would that not be taking rather a liberty?'

'It is a liberty only on *my* part, Mr. Argallo. I take it because it would help me. *I* can't be always thinking *only* of Ledgett.'

'Very well.'

My dear Max,—You must forgive me for not having thanked you sooner for your very pleasant letter. It came when I was stretched on a bed of sickness, suffering from a severe internal chill. I do not, however, regret that period of enforced rest, for it gave me the opportunity of reading once again, from first to last, *all* of Ledgett's books—besides the whole of that great album (which I once showed you) containing all that I have been able to collect of his not-republished work for the daily and weekly press. I found in this exercise a sovereign anodyne for pain. You know of old my feeling about Ledgett's work. Time has but intensified that passion, just as Time has deepened the genius of that man. Ledgett's later work is (not merely seems) his best. And yet, no! For who shall say the great wide-bosomed river is better than the little mountain-spring?

'Stop!' cried Argallo, and he read aloud the last sentence. 'Two lines of sheer blank verse! I don't like that at all.'

'Neither do I, Mr. Argallo. But there it is. I hope you don't think I did it through lack of ear? I did it to show how carried out of yourself you were at the moment of writing. Nature took the pen and wrote *for* you; and she's not, as we know, a very good writer. However, it's a small point: I'm quite ready to waive it. Put in *that* after *say*, and strike out *little* . . . So! Now let's finish up the letter. . . . No break in paragraph. You were too excited not to write straight on.'

And now I have a question to ask. Could you tell me whether there is any possibility of obtaining a scrap of Ledgett's MS? I have always refrained from writing to him—or rather (for I have written to him again and again) I have never posted any letter to him. To push and to pester is alien from my nature. Else, doubtless, I might be the possessor of many letters from L. I do in fact possess three, and they have always been among my most cherished possessions; but they are typewritten, circular letters— impersonal letters sent out, I conceive, to a great number of people. They are strong and cogent work, and not without that something of magic which is in everything that L. touches. (One of them, especially, about a luncheon to be offered at the Holborn Restaurant to the widow of an eminent Swedish novelist, is a masterpiece in its kind.) But they are *not enough*. 'I want, I want'—you remember that cry of Blake's?—a holograph letter written to some one person, and should deem it a bargain at whatever price the vendor might name.

Forgive me, dear Max, for troubling you.

Yours affectionately,

F. A.

'Or rather,' I added with a smile, 'forgive *me* for troubling *you*, Mr. Argallo. And accept my profoundest thanks.'

He rose from his table, and 'Believe me,' he said, 'the power to serve that poor man—if these letters *will* serve him, as you think—is the one good thing my—my wretched notoriety has brought me.'

'Ah, don't say that!—However,' I suggested, while I tore up the pages I had brought with me, 'since such work pleases you, you might write to me, from time to time, of your own accord, about Ledgett.'

He repeated the words 'from time to time,' and stood gazing down into the fire. There was silence while I took and folded and thrust into my pocketbook the letters already written. Suddenly, in a low voice, he broke this silence: 'There might then be many letters.' Still gazing into the fire, 'There might,' he said in a yet lower voice, 'be a long time for your friend to wait. My bodily health is sound.' I was about to speak when suddenly he looked at me, or rather through me and beyond me, in the strangest way. There had come into his eyes a light that I had never seen in them. There had come a look of veritable youth to his furrowed face. I could utter no word as he stood there strangely erect, soldierly—young. And it was in silence that I took my leave of him.

'Tragic,' a very apt word to describe Argallo's life, was the word that all the newspapers next morning used about his death. I, remembering what I had seen, knew better. However, the newspapers meant well. Their tributes to Argallo's genius in literature were whole-hearted; and on the ethical side they argued that, though the Almighty had set his canon against self-slaughter, their readers must remember that Argallo, wrongly no doubt, but honestly and with deep conviction, had held views of his own in the matter. One of the younger and more strenuous journals said that if the usual verdict were brought in by the Coroner's jury there would go up throughout the land such a howl of execration as would sweep away into limbo that whole fabric of 'Crowner's Quest Law' which had been a by-word and a mock ever since the days of the First Gravedigger in 'Hamlet,' and that such a verdict would moreover cause deep offence in Spain at a moment when it was vitally necessary for the peace of Europe that Spain and England should draw closer and yet closer together. I, of course, had to attend the inquest and give evidence; and I too (though rather for truth's and memory's sake than for Europe's) tried to avert the usual verdict. Asked whether Mr. Argallo had seemed to have anything on his mind, I said that he was a man who had always had much on his mind, and that my last impression of him was that he was exceptionally free from care or distress. The usual verdict was brought in, however. And I consoled myself with the reflection that it might make more acceptable to the Dean of Westminster the hasty but weighty petition that had been made to him. He, however, ran true to form. Argallo was buried, as Argallo would have wished, without official pomp.

He had made no will. But George Batford was of course the next of kin, and he told me that he would continue to devote his whole life to his uncle's service. This resolve, I inwardly foresaw, would entail vast exertions in the immediate future. Even the natural death of an eminent writer greatly intensifies, for a little while, the general desire to read him. The need for relays of new editions of Argallo's books would be specially urgent. Batford mentioned to me that all the translations would be issued 'shortly,' and that there would also be a folio edition of them, entitled 'The Wimbledon Edition.' 'And of course there's the "Life and Letters" to be done. I shall do that myself,' he said with a thrifty look. 'I'm not a practised hand, I know. But I wouldn't let the dear old gentleman's Life be written by any cold-blooded stranger. By the way, I suppose you've some letters from him?' I said that I had a few.

Within a month the newspapers had duly received and published a letter from the biographer saying that he would esteem it a favour if possessors of letters written by Felix Argallo would etc., etc. I would not of course lend the letters in my own possession until I had done some necessary spade-work on the mind of Ledgett. One is apt to postpone ticklish interviews, and, beautifully ingenuous though Ledgett was, and armed though I was with a Græco-medical word on which I placed great reliance, I had felt that my task might not be quite easy. But I hastened forth now to accomplish it. Woe to my old illusion that he was always at all his four clubs simultaneously!—he was not at the Savage. But I found him at the Authors'; and (good omen) he believed me that I had come just for the pleasure of his company. After we had sat talking for a while and were halfway through our whisky-and-soda, 'Sad, wasn't it,' I said, 'about Felix Argallo?'

'Dreadful! The greatest loss of our time. I'd give anything to bring that man back to life.'

'Ah. You feel that you rather neglected him?'

'No, not that. Hang it all, I've read every line— or almost every line—he ever wrote. But you mean I might have tried to organise some sort of——'

'No. Only I think perhaps you might have called on him again from time to time. He was a lonely man. And that one visit that you did pay him, all those years ago, at Penge,'—

'I? What years ago? What visit?'

'Oh, well, your life has been a very full one, of course. And in those days Argallo was an almost unknown writer. Still, I wonder that you have forgotten. *He* didn't forget. Nor did W. E. Henley, I'll wager. Don't you remember that Henley was there that day?'

'He couldn't have been. I mean *I* couldn't have been. I never once met him. I did once, when he was living at Muswell Hill, go to see him about something. But he was out.'

'Perhaps when Argallo introduced you to him that day at Penge, you didn't catch his name?'

'But I tell you,' said Ledgett, flushed and almost angry, 'I never set eyes on Argallo.'

'Curious. Very curious. You don't remember dining with me, to meet him, at the little Solferino restaurant? I myself forget the exact date. But it must have been early in February, '98. You and he and I, nobody else. We were at that corner table—don't you remember?—to the left. You did most of the talking. You were in great form that night. But I gather you were in still greater when you went down to Penge.'

'But—look here! You must have got some sort of—hallucination.'

'Strange that Argallo should have shared it with me, Ledgett.' I had drawn out my pocket-book, and I now selected from its contents the first of Argallo's letters. 'This,' I said, handing it over, 'may help you to recall things.'

His mind worked in obviously feverish confusion as he pored over the script. 'Look here!' he said to me at last. 'Somebody must have impersonated me!'

'You mean that *you* would never have said you thought my work extremely promising?'

'No—I think it is. I mean, I like it immensely, but——'

'If anybody did impersonate you, Ledgett—and frankly I don't see why anybody should—his face must have resembled yours exactly. Argallo had various photographs of you—reproductions of them, at least. He cut them out of newspapers, he kept them in an album, with the articles that you wrote. He knew your whole face—forehead and chin and

everything—by heart. He often showed me the
album. He mentions it in one of the other letters
about you.'

'He wrote other letters about me? I mean
about——'

'The second one is more about your work than
about you.' I passed it on to him.

'I never,' he said after a while, huskily, 'I never
could have believed—that such a man—that my
stuff——'

'Well, those were his feelings, anyhow. Let's see:
the third letter is of a more personal kind. But he
speaks of your work on the last page, I think, yes.'

Presently, as he read, the veins stood out upon his
temples. He was so bewildered that I felt quite guilty.
But there could be no going back. I had to carry the
good work—Argallo's and mine—through.

'Well?' I said, meeting his gaze sardonically. 'The
mystic impersonator again? Or what?'

'Surely,' he gasped, 'you didn't believe, when you
got this letter, that *I* was the——'

'My dear fellow, it was none of my business. I dismissed the matter from my mind.'

'But you don't seriously believe it *was* me?'

I laughingly lit a cigarette. Ledgett pressed his
question.

'I know nothing about it, my dear fellow. I simply
think you may have forgotten.'

'How could I forget a thing of that kind?'

'Well, it rather depends on how many things of
that kind have happened to you. I take it that you
aren't a misogynist. You could hardly have evolved

all the delightful heroines of your novels without a fairly—or call it a terribly—wide experience. Cast your mind back. May the 4th, 1904. What were you doing on the afternoon of that day?'

'How on earth should I know?'

'You weren't keeping a diary in that year?'

'No. I've never kept a diary.'

'That in itself looks fishy. But come, man!—jog your wretched memory and then be quite frank with me! An afternoon in May—an elm tree—two green chairs under it. Do these things suggest *nothing* to you?'

'Oh, I don't say I've never had an appointment with a girl in a park. But never with—with *that* kind of girl.'

'You wouldn't have *kept* an appointment with that kind?'

'I don't say that.'

'Ah, Ledgett, Ledgett!'

'What I do say is that I should remember about it.'

'As clearly, perhaps, as you remember that evening at the Solferino, and that long day at Penge?'

He looked at me with dazed eyes.

'Don't worry,' I said. 'Your mind is all right—in all other ways, I'm quite sure. You've only got monoutinosamnesia.'

'What's that?'

'Oh, a very common thing. I've heard of heaps of cases of it. The word means "forgetfulness of some one thing." Just as some people are always remembering some one thing, others permanently forget some one thing. Doctors say it's due to some infinitesimal lesion in the brain.'

'Then I'd better go straight to some good doctor.'

'Don't do that. Sheer waste of time. Such lesions can't be cured—any more than they can be accounted for. And they have no effect on the rest of the brain. They're secerned.'

'Secerned?'

'Yes, to all intents and purposes they are. But of course,' I was careful to add, 'they have what's called enviroactivity.'

'What's that?'

'It means that the patient—I mean the man—not only forgets some one thing, but also forgets everything connected with it. You, for example, remember nothing connected with Argallo.'

'Surely,' said Ledgett, with a dangerous gleam of intelligence, 'his books are connected with him? Yet I remember *them* well enough.'

'You do. Yes. That's so. . . . But his books aren't connected with his actual physical presence; and it's that presence which is the some one thing in your case. Anything that you saw when you were *in* that presence is blotted out. You remember having been in the Solferino at various times; but the Solferino with Argallo in it eludes you—and so do I, your attentive host there. The little house at Penge, too, the listening Henley, that old elm tree in the Park, that poor lady—all gone irrevocably, Ledgett, all snatched away forever by enviroactivity.'

'But,' my friend had a second gleam, 'if I really did go and meet that lady, I must have met her before somewhere. Why should I forget that?'

'*Have* you forgotten it, Ledgett? Honour bright? Well, I'll believe you. Enviroactivity often effaces previous events. And subsequent ones too. I daresay you don't remember whether or not she did persecute you. Strange, isn't it? Stranger than anything in all your novels.'

'Yes, it's stranger than anything I could have imagined.'

'And somehow ridiculous, too. I wouldn't tell anybody about it, if I were you. You see, when these letters of Argallo's are published they'll make rather an impression on people. And if you went around saying you didn't remember him, people would wonder. You wouldn't want to say, "The fact is, I'm a monoutinosamnesiac." And without that explanation people might think you rather heartless. By the way, talking of supposed heartlessness, would you rather I didn't send in that third letter?'

Ledgett, who had one elbow on the arm of his chair, raised one hand to his forehead. I had never seen him do that. 'It is a very fine letter in itself,' he said, with deliberation. 'Finely felt and finely expressed. To keep it back would hardly be loyal, Beerbohm, to our friend's memory.' I asked whether he would prefer that two strokes should be substituted for his name. He said firmly that it would not be right to tamper with anything. He removed his hand from his forehead and held it out for the fourth letter. 'Anything personal in this one?' he asked.

'No, I'm afraid there isn't. But it's a very nice letter. It's finely felt and finely expressed. And I believe it's the last letter he wrote to anybody.'

'It's the greatest tribute,' Ledgett presently said, 'ever paid to my work.' And he nursed his chin.

Nor, when I rose to go, did he rise and see me off the premises. He shook hands with me from his chair.

However, I posted the letters, to George Batford, that evening.

Next day, full of a happy inspiration, I went to a second-hand bookseller in the Charing Cross Road. The craze for first editions of modern authors had already, in a small way, begun; and I had an inkling that it would grow—though I no more foresaw the vast dimensions it would attain than I foresaw the War that for a time stopped its growth. While I gave my order to the bookseller, I expected to reap ultimately a fair profit, but nothing grandiose.

Meanwhile, the principal publishers strove fiercely with one another for acquisition of the Life and Letters; and the 'advance' paid to George Batford by the victor was commensurate with the fury of the fray. The two handsome volumes were out early in November. The victor advertised them as one of the greatest of English biographies, and also as an ideal gift-book for the Christmas Season. To me it seemed that George's nepotic piety did not atone for certain drawbacks. I found in his work a lack of discernment, style, and lucid order. Of course he had been heavily handicapped. Very little was known of Argallo's early exploits in Spain; very little had happened to him in Penge, before the boom; practically nothing had happened to him in Wimbledon, before the end. But George's innumerable long quotations from

Tuckman's 'History of the Carlist Wars,' and from the Rev. J. F. Copley's book about the antiquities of Penge, and from several books about the topography of Wimbledon, were not in themselves interesting, had not been well-chosen; and his history of the boom, with some eighty reviews of 'Last Shadows' quoted verbatim from the English and American press, was a dreadful muddle. Nor was he better in touching the personal note. The last chapter—from its opening words—'I will now attempt a pen-picture of my Uncle when I first saw him. He was very tall in heighth with a dark Spanish complexion which showed his Spanish blood on the father's side, and spoke in a low sort of voice,' to its closing words, 'But his memory lives in the remembrance of all the English-speaking public both of the British Empire and America'—was a singularly infelicitous piece of writing. Argallo's own letters were the one strong point in the book. True, he had written few in his later age; and of his early letters few had been preserved. But there was a general agreement among the critics that he was certainly in the foremost rank of English letter-writers. This opinion I shared. I found Argallo's letters very splendid. I was therefore surprised that by several critics the four letters addressed to myself were singled out as among the most characteristic and the best.

And there was another thing that rather took me aback. I had supposed that the revelation of Argallo's feeling about Ledgett's work would violently flutter the dove-cots. There was not the stirring of a wing. There was but a bland cooing. 'It is pleasant to find

that he was among the first to appreciate the genius
of Mr. Walter Ledgett.'—'He gives us the penetrat-
ing criticism that can be had only from a master-
craftsman. What he wrote about Browning in his
youth is hardly less fine than his later appreciations
of Joseph Conrad, of D'Annunzio, and of Walter
Ledgett.'—'The dark beads of his later years are
strung on the golden thread of his generous passion
for Ledgett's work.' Absurd as it may seem, even I,
knowing what I knew, was beguiled by the melodious
chorus, and did not wonder that Ledgett's manner,
whenever I came across him, was so off-hand as to
be not even patronising. From many people Argallo's
'Max' received an unwonted deference. But how
should Argallo's idol be one of these?

I was told that to such people as the Bishop who
put him up for The Athenæum, and the Field-
Marshal who seconded him, his manner was fairly
cordial. But when, in the following Spring, he was
elected under Rule 2, he did not forgather much with
the literary members. From his other clubs he had
resigned soon after my chat with him at the Authors'.
His old friends, behaving to him in the old way, had
given him deep offence, and at the Savage especially
he had made some unpleasant scenes. Even at The
Athenæum, I heard, his temper was by no means
equable. He was reported to have been unjustifiably
caustic to an eminent old scientist who had said that
it must be a great satisfaction to him to have been
esteemed so highly by such a man as Felix Argallo.
Stupendous though the sales of his books now were,
and undisputed though his genius was by even the

most acrid young persons, he did not appear to be a contented man. Oxford, always rather slow in the uptake, did not offer him a Doctorate of Letters that Summer. He very wrongly took this as a personal slight. Argallo's letter to Lord Curzon (May, 1907), begging to decline that high honour, was a noble and touching document, a classic letter. But I would barter its existence to have seen Ledgett turn on his heel, as he did, one day in the Autumn of 1913, when Lord Curzon came towards him, with outstretched hand, in the library of The Athenæum. In 1914, you will remember, Oxford did the correct thing; but all who attended the Encaenia agreed that Valterius Ledgett looked very sulky, very stern and unbending, in his scarlet gown.

I have always loved Oxford. I welcomed, as a sign of her undiminished power, the fact that Ledgett's Doctorate sent up by ten points the market-price of 'Ledgett Firsts.' I wondered whether this were the moment to 'unload.' I was greatly tempted. Even one of Ledgett's books, despite the spell his fame had cast on me, was more than I really wanted. It was awful to have to go on harbouring two 'clean copies' of the first edition of everything he had proliferated. My sleuth-hound of the Charing Cross Road had carried out my order with appalling thoroughness. I had two clean copies of every brochure that Ledgett had written in his youth for the lesser railway-companies, for keepers of seaside hotels, for keepers of hotels inland, for heaven knows whom. I had two clean copies of every song for which he had written words. And *what* words! Surely I should unload now? 'Not yet,' whispered my wiser self. 'The market price for Firsts is nothing to what it will yet be. And every year of Ledgett's life will send up Ledgett's value.' Two months later came the War; and one forgot everything else.

Even Ledgett was forgotten. Practically no notice was taken of the sonnet in which he expressed his envy of Youth, and his regret that he personally could not go out 'And fight the accurséd Kaiser face to face.' The continuance of the War weighed heavily on him. He did not go so far as to try to stop it, but, as he said to me one day when I met him in Pall Mall, he felt that 'this total abeyance of the things of the mind' was in itself a great danger to the country. The air-raids, I think, he took as a personal insult. Anyway, before the end of 1915, he retired to Wordsworth's Windermere. And one likes to think of him there among the unbombed Lakes, reading his own books incessantly. When the War was over, the things of the mind were remembered. John Bull sat down to feast on them with the appetite of a starved man. Ledgett's name shone now the more lustrously for its long occlusion. Ledgett Firsts rose 15 points above pre-war value. Should I unload now? But again my wiser self restrained me.

Not long after the Armistice, I went to Italy, where I had mostly lived, for a while before the War; and in Italy I now settled. A few days before my departure I had a glimpse—my last—of Ledgett. He was walking towards The Athenæum—walking very slowly, leaning heavily on a stick, for he had become, in spite of the food-restrictions of the past years, enormously fat. Too intense contemplation of his own genius had begun to undermine his health, I was sure. His face was flabby, and his eyes were lack-lustre. I did not foresee that his naturally strong constitution would preserve him for eight more years.

Happening to have come over from Italy a fort-night ago, I attended, of course, the service in the Abbey last Tuesday. I was glad to be able to pay this last tribute to my friend's memory. I was glad also, on the following day, to hear that Mr. Nat Heinz, the famous 'Firsts Agent', had recently come over from New York on one of his periodical visits to London, and was staying at the Ritz. I wrote at once a respectful note to this magnoperator, telling him that if he would do me the honour to call on me at the Charing Cross Hotel I could show him some things that might interest him. I then drove to the storage warehouse that harboured the packing-case in which were my duplicated copies of Ledgett Firsts. This possession I transported to my hotel and, with a view to the magnoperator, dashingly engaged a private sitting-room. There, yesterday morning, with my baits outspread on two tables, three chairs and a sofa, I awaited the hour fixed by Mr. Heinz for his visit. I was prepared for a man with a cool, depreciative manner. Such a manner is essential to such men's business. But the small dark eyes of Mr. Heinz, as they alighted on treasure after treasure, gave forth uncontrollable gleams.

Between the pages of some of the books were
insertions of what is called 'relative matter.' There
were letters that I had received from Ledgett at
various dates, there were *menus* that had been handed
round after convivial dinners and signed by diners
of whom Ledgett was one, there were several sketches
of Ledgett made by Phil May. I especially drew Mr.
Heinz's attention to the books in which I had inserted
my four letters from Argallo. But I had set overmuch
store on these. 'Ar-*what?*' said Mr. Heinz. 'Oh,
Argallo; yes; I reckle-ect. The author who took his
own life. I handled Argallo wares extens'vely at one
time. They've greatly dee-preciated.'

He made, however, no other cavils. And he presently drew, without a murmur, a cheque for the
amount that I firmly named to him. With this in my
pocket, I lunched heartily, but, before going forth
from my hotel to pay it into my bank, I told the young
lady at the bureau that I should not need my private
sitting-room any more. The bank-clerk who received
my cheque, and knew my affairs, saw through my
assumption of languor instantly and gave me a very
human smile of congratulation.

On my way back to Charing Cross, I met a friend
and fellow-writer who is noted for his acumen in
matters of business; and, to impress him, I poured
forth the story of my transaction.

He gave a sharp whistle. 'My dear good fool,
you've put nine hundred pounds into Nat Heinz's
pocket!'

'Well, after all,' I reasoned with him, 'that's
exactly the sum he put into *my* pocket. So we're

quits. I never want to get the better of anybody. Enough that for once Europe has held her own!'

'But she hasn't!' my friend retorted. 'America has got the books!'

This, I confessed, was a point I hadn't thought of. But perhaps also it is a point which Mr. Heinz's clients, when these pages shall have appeared, won't think very much of.

'SAVONAROLA' BROWN

'SAVONAROLA' BROWN

1917

I LIKE to remember that I was the first to call him so, for, though he always deprecated the nickname, in his heart he was pleased by it, I know, and encouraged to go on.

Quite apart from its significance, he had reason to welcome it. He had been unfortunate at the font. His parents, at the time of his birth, lived in Ladbroke Crescent, W. They must have been an extraordinarily unimaginative couple, for they could think of no better name for their child than Ladbroke. This was all very well for him till he went to school. But you can fancy the indignation and delight of us boys at finding among us a new-comer, who on his own confession, had been named after a Crescent. I don't know how it is nowadays, but thirty-five years ago, certainly, schoolboys regarded the possession of *any* Christian name as rather unmanly. As we all had these encumbrances, we had to wreak our scorn on any one who was cumbered in a queer fashion. I myself, bearer of a Christian name adjudged eccentric though brief, had had much to put up with in my first term. Brown's arrival, therefore, at the beginning of my second term, was a good thing for me, and I am afraid I was very prominent among his persecutors. Trafalgar Brown, Tottenham Court Brown, Bond Brown—what names did we little brutes *not* cull for him from the London Directory? Except how miserable we made his life, I do not remember much about him as he was at that time, and the only important part of the little else that I do recall is that already he showed a strong sense for literature. For the majority of us Carthusians, literature was bounded on the north by Whyte Melville, on the south by Hawley Smart, on the east by the former, and on the west by the latter. Little Brown used to read Harrison Ainsworth, Wilkie Collins, and other writers whom we, had we assayed them, would have dismissed as 'deep.' It has been said by Mr. Arthur Symons that 'all art is a mode of escape.' The art of letters did not, however, enable Brown to escape so far from us as he would have wished. In my third term he did not reappear among us. His parents had in some sort atoned. Unimaginative though they were, it seems they could understand a tale of woe laid before them circumstantially, and had engaged a private tutor for their boy. Fifteen years elapsed before I saw him again.

This was at the second night of some play. I was dramatic critic for the *Saturday Review*, and, weary of meeting the same lot of people over and over again at first nights, had recently sent a circular to the managers asking that I might have seats for second nights instead. I found that there existed as distinct and invariable a lot of second-nighters as of first-nighters. The second-nighters were less 'showy'; but then, they came rather to see than to be seen, and there was an air, that I liked, of earnestness and hopefulness about them. I used to write a great deal about the future of the British drama, and they, for their part, used to think and talk a great deal about it. People who care about books and pictures find much to interest and please them in the present. It is only the students of the theatre who always fall back, or rather forward, on the future. Though second-nighters do come to see, they remain rather to hope and pray. I should have known anywhere, by the visionary look in his eyes, that Brown was a con-firmed second-nighter.

What surprises me is that I knew he was Brown. It is true that he had not grown much in those fifteen years: his brow was still disproportionate to his body, and he looked young to have become 'confirmed' in any habit. But it is also true that not once in the past ten years, at any rate, had he flitted through my mind and poised on my conscience.

I hope that I and those other boys had long ago ceased from recurring to him in nightmares. Cordial though the hand was that I offered him, and highly civilised my whole demeanour, he seemed afraid that at any moment I might begin to dance around him, shooting out my lips at him and calling him Seven-Sisters Brown or something of that kind. It was only after constant meetings at second nights, and in-numerable *entr'acte* talks about the future of the drama, that he began to trust me. In course of time we formed the habit of walking home together as far as Cumberland Place, at which point our ways diverged. I gathered that he was still living with his parents, but he did not tell me where, for they had not, as I learned by reference to the Red Book, moved from Ladbroke Crescent.

I found his company restful rather than inspiring. His days were spent in clerkship at one of the smaller Government Offices, his evenings—except when there was a second night—in reading and writing. He did not seem to know much, or to wish to know more, about life. Books and plays, first editions and second nights, were what he cared for. On matters of religion and ethics he was as little keen as he seemed to be on human character in the raw; so that (though I had already suspected him of writing, or meaning to write, a play) my eyebrows did rise when he told me he meant to write a play about Savonarola.

He made me understand, however, that it was rather the name than the man that had first attracted him. He said that the name was in itself a great incentive to blank-verse. He uttered it to me slowly, in a voice so much deeper than his usual voice, that I nearly laughed. For the actual bearer of the name he had no hero-worship, and said it was by a mere accident that he had chosen him as central figure. He had thought of writing a tragedy about Sardana-palus; but the volume of the 'Encyclopædia Britannica' in which he was going to look up the main facts about Sardanapalus happened to open at Savonarola. Hence a sudden and complete peripety in the student's mind. He told me he had read the Encyclo-pædia's article carefully, and had dipped into one or two of the books there mentioned as authorities. He seemed almost to wish he hadn't. 'Facts get in one's way so,' he complained. 'History is one thing, drama is another. Aristotle said drama was more philosophic than history because it showed us what

men *would* do, not just what they *did*. I think that's
so true, don't you? I want to show what Savonarola
would have done if—' He paused.

'If what?'

'Well, that's just the point. I haven't settled that
yet. When I've thought of a plot, I shall go straight
ahead.'

I said that I supposed he intended his tragedy
rather for the study than for the stage. This seemed
to hurt him. I told him that what I meant was that
managers always shied at anything without 'a strong
feminine interest.' This seemed to worry him. I
advised him not to think about managers. He promised that he would think only about Savonarola.

I know now that this promise was not exactly kept
by him; and he may have felt slightly awkward when,
some weeks later, he told me he had begun the play.
'I've hit on an initial idea,' he said, 'and that's
enough to start with. I gave up my notion of invent-
ing a plot in advance. I thought it would be a mistake.
I don't want puppets on wires. I want Savonarola to
work out his destiny in his own way. Now that I have
the initial idea, what I've got to do is to make Savonarola *live*. I hope I shall be able to do this. Once he's
alive, I shan't interfere with him. I shall just watch
him. Won't it be interesting? He isn't alive yet. But
there's plenty of time. You see, he doesn't come on at
the rise of the curtain. A Friar and a Sacristan come
on and talk about him. By the time they've finished,
perhaps he'll be alive. But they won't have finished
yet. Not that they're going to say very much. But I
write slowly.'

I remember the mild thrill I had when, one evening, he took me aside and said in an undertone, 'Savonarola has come on. Alive!' For me the MS. hereinafter printed has an interest that for you it cannot have, so a-bristle am I with memories of the meetings I had with its author throughout the nine years he took over it. He never saw me without reporting progress, or lack of progress. Just what was going on, or standing still, he did not divulge. After the entry of Savonarola, he never told me what characters were appearing. 'All sorts of people appear,' he would say rather helplessly. 'They insist. I can't prevent them.' I used to say it must be great fun to be a creative artist; but at this he always shook his head: 'I don't create. *They* do. Savonarola especially, of course. I just look on and record. I never know what's going to happen next.' He had the advantage of me in knowing at any rate what had happened last. But whenever I pled for a glimpse he would again shake his head:

'The thing *must* be judged as a whole. Wait till I've come to the end of the Fifth Act.'

So impatient did I grow that, as the years went by, I used rather to resent his presence at second nights. I felt he ought to be at his desk. His, I used to tell him, was the only drama whose future ought to concern him now. And in point of fact he had, I think, lost the true spirit of the second-nighter, and came rather to be seen than to see. He liked the knowledge that here and there in the auditorium, when he entered it, some one would be saying 'Who is that?' and receiving the answer 'Oh, don't you know?

That's "Savonarola" Brown.' This sort of thing, however, did not make him cease to be the modest, unaffected fellow I had known. He always listened to the advice I used to offer him, though inwardly he must have chafed at it. Myself a fidgety and un-inspired person, unable to begin a piece of writing before I know just how it shall end, I had always been afraid that sooner or later Brown would take some turning that led nowhither—would lose him-self and come to grief. This fear crept into my glad-ness when, one evening in the spring of 1909, he told me he had finished the Fourth Act. Would he win out safely through the Fifth?

He himself was looking rather glum; and, as we walked away from the theatre, I said to him, 'I suppose you feel rather like Thackeray when he'd "killed the Colonel": you've got to kill the Monk.'

'Not quite that,' he answered. 'But of course he'll die very soon now. A couple of years or so. And it does seem rather sad. It's not merely that he's so full of life. He has been becoming much more *human* lately. At first I only respected him. Now I have a real affection for him.'

This was an interesting glimpse at last, but I turned from it to my besetting fear.

'Haven't you,' I asked, 'any notion of *how* he is to die?'

Brown shook his head.

'But in a tragedy,' I insisted, 'the catastrophe *must* be led up to, step by step. My dear Brown, the end of the hero *must* be logical and rational.'

'I don't see that,' he said, as we crossed Piccadilly Circus. 'In actual life it isn't so. What is there to prevent a motor-omnibus from knocking me over and killing me at this moment?'

At that moment, by what has always seemed to me the strangest of coincidences, and just the sort of thing that playwrights ought to avoid, a motor-omnibus knocked Brown over and killed him.

He had, as I afterwards learned, made a will in which he appointed me his literary executor. Thus passed into my hands the unfinished play by whose name he had become known to so many people.

I hate to say that I was disappointed in it, but I had better confess quite frankly that, on the whole, I was. Had Brown written it quickly and read it to me soon after our first talk about it, it might in some ways have exceeded my hopes. But he had become for me, by reason of that quiet and unhasting devotion to his work while the years came and went, a sort of a hero; and the very mystery involving just what he was about had addicted me to those ideas of magnificence which the unknown is said always to foster.

Even so, however, I am not blind to the great merits of the play as it stands. It is well that the writer of poetic drama should be a dramatist and a poet. Here is a play that abounds in striking situations, and I have searched it vainly for one line that does not scan. What I nowhere feel is that I have not elsewhere been thrilled or lulled by the same kind of thing. I do not go so far as to say that Brown inherited his parents' deplorable lack of imagination. But I do wish he had been less sensitive than he was to impressions, or else had seen and read fewer poetic dramas ancient and modern. Remembering that visionary look in his eyes, remembering that he was as displeased as I by the work of all living playwrights, and as dissatisfied with the great efforts of the Elizabethans, I wonder that he was not more immune from influences.

Also, I cannot but wish still that he had faltered in his decision to make no scenario. There is much to be said for the theory that a dramatist should first vitalise his characters and then leave them unfettered; but I do feel that Brown's misused the confidence he reposed in them. The labour of so many years has somewhat the air of being a mere improvisation. Savonarola himself, after the First Act or so, strikes me as utterly inconsistent. It may be that he is just complex, like Hamlet. He does in the Fourth Act show traces of that Prince. I suppose this is why he struck Brown as having become 'more human.' To me he seems merely a poorer creature.

But enough of these reservations. In my anxiety for poor Brown's sake that you should not be disappointed, perhaps I have been carrying tactfulness too far and prejudicing you against that for which I specially want your favour. Here, without more ado, is—

'SAVONAROLA'

A Tragedy

By
L. BROWN

ACT I

SCENE: *A Room in the Monastery of San Marco,
Florence.*
TIME: 1490, A.D. *A summer morning.*

Enter the SACRISTAN *and a* FRIAR.

SACR.
Savonarola looks more grim to-day
Than ever. Should I speak my mind, I'd say
That he was fashioning some new great scourge
To flay the backs of men.

FRI.
               'Tis even so.
Brother Filippo saw him stand last night
In solitary vigil till the dawn
Lept o'er the Arno, and his face was such
As men may wear in Purgatory—nay,
E'en in the inmost core of Hell's own fires.

SACR.
I often wonder if some woman's face,
Seen at some rout in his old worldling days,

Haunts him e'en now, e'en here, and urges him
To fierier fury 'gainst the Florentines.

FRI.
Savonarola love-sick! Ha, ha, ha!
Love-sick? He, love-sick? 'Tis a goodly jest?
The *con*firm'd misogyn a ladies' man!
Thou must have eaten of some strange red herb
That takes the reason captive. I will swear
Savonarola never yet hath seen
A woman but he spurn'd her. Hist! He comes.

[*Enter* SAVONAROLA, *rapt in thought*.]

Give thee good morrow, Brother.

SACR.

      And therewith
A multitude of morrows equal-good
Till thou, by Heaven's grace, hast wrought the work
Nearest thine heart.

SAV.

    I thank thee, Brother, yet
I thank thee not, for that my thankfulness
(An such there be) gives thanks to Heav'n alone.

FRI. [*To* SACR.]
'Tis a right answer he hath given thee.
Had Sav'narola spoken less than thus,
Methinks me, the less Sav'narola he.
As when the snow lies on yon Apennines.
White as the hem of Mary Mother's robe,
And insusceptible to the sun's rays,
Being harder to the touch than temper'd steel,

E'en so this great gaunt monk white-visagèd
Upstands to Heaven and to Heav'n devotes
The scarpèd thoughts that crown the upper slopes
Of his abrupt and *aus*tere nature.

SACR.

Aye.

[*Enter* LUCREZIA BORGIA, ST. FRANCIS OF ASSISI, *and* LEONARDO DA VINCI. LUC, *is thickly veiled.*]

ST. FRAN.
This is the place.

LUC. [*Pointing at* SAV.]
                    And this the man! [*Aside.*] And I—
By the hot blood that courses i' my veins
I swear it ineluctably—the woman!

SAV.
Who is this wanton?

  [LUC. *throws back her hood, revealing her face.*
  SAV. *starts back, gazing at her.*]

ST. FRAN.
                    Hush, Sir! 'Tis my little sister
The poisoner, right well-belov'd by all
Whom she as yet hath spared. Hither she came
Mounted upon another little sister of mine—
A mare, caparison'd in goodly wise.
She—I refer now to Lucrezia—
Desireth to have word of thee anent
Some matter that befrets her.

SAV. [*To* LUC.]

Hence! Begone!
Savonarola will not tempted be
By face of woman e'en tho' 't be, tho' 'tis,
Surpassing fair. All hope abandon therefore.
I charge thee: Vade retro, Satanas!

LEONARDO.
Sirrah, thou speakst in haste, as is the way
Of monkish men. The beauty of Lucrezia
Commends, not discommends, her to the eyes
Of keener thinkers than I take thee for.
I am an artist and an engineer,
Giv'n o'er to subtile dreams of what shall be
On this our planet. I foresee a day
When men shall skim the earth i' certain chairs
Not drawn by horses but sped on by oil
Or other matter, and shall thread the sky
Birdlike.

LUC.

It may be as thou sayest, friend,
Or may be not. [*To* SAV.] As touching this our errand,
I crave of thee, Sir Monk, an audience
Instanter.

FRI.

Lo! Here Alighieri comes.
I had methought me he was still at Parma.

[*Enter* DANTE.]

ST. FRAN. [*To* DAN.]
How fares my little sister Beatrice?

DAN.
She died, alack, last sennight.

ST. FRAN.
                              Did she so?
If the condolences of men avail
Thee aught, take mine.

DAN.
                        They are of no avail.

SAV. [*To* LUC.]
I do refuse thee audience.

LUC.
                              Then why
Didst thou not say so promptly when I ask'd it?

SAV.
Full well thou knowst that I was interrupted
By Alighieri's entry.

   [*Noise without. Enter Guelfs and Ghibellines
   fighting.*]
                        What is this?

LUC.
I did not think that in this cloister'd spot
There would be so much doing. I had look'd
To find Savonarola all alone
And tempt him in his uneventful cell. .
Instead o' which—Spurn'd am I? I am I.
There was a time, Sir, look to 't! O damnation!
What is 't? Anon then! These my toys, my gauds,
That in the cradle—aye, 't my mother's breast—
I puled and lisped at,—'Tis impossible,

Tho', faith, 'tis not so, forasmuch as 'tis.
And I a daughter of the Borgias!—
Or so they told me. Liars! Flatterers!
Currying lick-spoons! Where's the Hell of 't then?
'Tis time that I were going. Farewell, Monk,
But I'll avenge me ere the sun has sunk.

> [*Exeunt* LUC., ST. FRAN., *and* LEONARDO,
> *followed by* DAN. SAV., *having watched* LUC.
> *out of sight, sinks to his knees, sobbing.* FRI. *and*
> SACR. *watch him in amazement. Guelfs and*
> *Ghibellines continue fighting as the Curtain falls.*]

ACT II

TIME: *Afternoon of same day.*
SCENE: *Lucrezia's Laboratory. Retorts, test-tubes,
etc. On small Renaissance table, up C., is a great
poison-bowl, the contents of which are being stirred by
the* FIRST APPRENTICE. *The* SECOND APPRENTICE
stands by, watching him.

SECOND APP.
For whom is the brew destin'd?

FIRST APP.
                       I know not.
Lady Lucrezia did but lay on me
Injunctions as regards the making of 't,
The which I have obey'd. It is compounded
Of a malignant and a deadly weed
Found not save in the Gulf of Spezia,
And one small phial of 't, I am advis'd,
Were more than 'nough to slay a regiment
Of Messer Malatesta's condottieri
In all their armour.

SECOND APP.
                 I can well believe it.
Mark how the purple bubbles froth upon
The evil surface of its nether slime!

[Enter LUC.]

LUC. [*To* FIRST APP.]
Is 't done, Sir Sluggard?

FIRST APP.

                 Madam, to a turn.

LUC.
Had it not been so, I with mine own hand
Would have outpour'd it down thy gullet, knave.
See, here's a ring of cunningly-wrought gold
That I, on a dark night, did purchase from
A goldsmith on the Ponte Vecchio.
Small was his shop, and hoar of visage he.
I did bemark that from the ceiling's beams
Spiders had spun their webs for many a year,
The which hung erst like swathes of gossamer
Seen in the shadows of a fairy glade,
But now most woefully were weighted o'er
With gather'd dust. Look well now at the ring!
Touch'd here, behold, it opes a cavity
Capacious of three drops of yon fell stuff.
Dost heed? Whoso then puts it on his finger
Dies, and his soul is from his body rapt
To Hell or Heaven as the case may be.
Take thou this toy and pour the three drops in.

[Hands ring to FIRST APP. *and comes down* C.]

So, Sav'narola, thou shalt learn that I
Utter no threats but I do make them good.
Ere this day's sun hath wester'd from the view
Thou art to preach from out the Loggia
Dei Lanzi to the cits in the Piazza.
I, thy Lucrezia, will be upon the steps
To offer thee with phrases seeming-fair
That which shall seal thine eloquence for ever.

O mighty lips that held the world in spell
But would not meet these little lips of mine
In the sweet way that lovers use—O thin,
Cold, tight-drawn, bloodless lips, which natheless I
Deem of all lips the most magnifical
In this our city——

[*Enter the Borgias'* FOOL.]

Well, Fool, what's thy latest?

FOOL

Aristotle's or Zeno's, Lady—'tis neither latest nor
last. For, marry, if the cobbler stuck to his last, then
were his latest his last *in rebus ambulantibus*. Argal,
I stick at nothing but cobble-stones, which, by the
same token, are stuck to the road by men's fingers.

LUC.

How many crows may nest in a grocer's jerkin?

FOOL

A full dozen at cock-crow, and something less under
the dog-star, by reason of the dew, which lies heavy
on men taken by the scurvy.

LUC. [*To* FIRST APP.]

Methinks the Fool is a fool.

FOOL

And therefore, by auricular deduction, am I own
twin to the Lady Lucrezia!

[*Sings.*]

When pears hang green on the garden wall
    With a nid, and a nod, and a niddy-niddy-o

Then prank you, lads and lasses all
    With a yea and a nay and a niddy-o.

But when the thrush flies out o' the frost
    With a nid, [*etc.*]
'Tis time for loons to count the cost,
    With a yea [*etc.*]

[*Enter the* PORTER.]

PORTER
O my dear Mistress, there is one below
Demanding to have instant word of thee.
I told him that your Ladyship was not
At home. Vain perjury! He would not take
Nay for an answer.

LUC.
           Ah? What manner of man
Is he?

PORTER
    A personage the like of whom
Is wholly unfamiliar to my gaze
Cowl'd is he, but I saw his great eyes glare
From their deep sockets in such wise as leopards
Glare from their caverns, crouching ere they spring
On their reluctant prey.

LUC.
           And what name gave he?

PORTER [*After a pause.*]
Something-arola.

Luc.

Savon-? [Porter *nods*.] Show him up.
[*Exit* Porter.]

Fool

If he be right astronomically, Mistress, then is he the greater dunce in respect of true learning, the which goes by the globe. Argal, 'twere better he widened his wind-pipe.

[*Sings.*]

Fly home, sweet self,
Nothing's for weeping,
Hemp was not made
For lovers' keeping,
Lovers' keeping,
Cheerly, cheerly, fly away.

Hew no more wood
While ash is glowing,
The longest grass
Is lovers' mowing,
Lovers' mowing,
Cheerly, [*etc.*]

[*Re-enter* Porter, *followed by* Sav. *Exeunt* Porter, Fool, *and* First *and* Second Apps.]

Sav.

I am no more a monk, I am a man
O' the world.

[*Throws off cowl and frock, and stands forth in the costume of a Renaissance nobleman.* Lucrezia *looks him up and down.*]

Luc.

          Thou cutst a sorry figure.

Sav.

                          That
Is neither here nor there. I love you, Madam.

Luc.
And this, methinks, is neither there nor here,
For that my love of thee hath vanishèd,
Seeing thee thus beprankt. Go pad thy calves!
Thus mightst thou, just conceivably, with luck
Capture the fancy of some serving-wench.

Sav.
And this is all thou hast to say to me?

Luc.
It is.

Sav.

       I am dismiss'd?

Luc.

                 Thou art.

Sav.

                       'Tis well.

                  [Resumes frock and cowl.]

Savonarola is himself once more.

Luc.
And all my love for him returns to me
A thousandfold!

SAV.

              Too late! My pride of manhood
Is wounded irremediably. I'll
To the Piazza, where my flock awaits me.
Thus do we see that men make great mistakes
But may amend them when the conscience wakes.

                                 [*Exit.*]

LUC.

I'm half avengèd now, but only half:
'Tis with the ring I'll have the final laugh!
Tho' love be sweet, revenge is sweeter far.
To the Piazza! Ha, ha, ha, ha, har!

> [*Seizes ring, and exit. Through open door are
> heard, as the Curtain falls, sounds of a terrific
> hubbub in the Piazza.*]

ACT III

Scene: *The Piazza.*

Time: *A few minutes anterior to close of preceding Act.*

The Piazza is filled from end to end with a vast seething crowd that is drawn entirely from the lower orders. There is a sprinkling of wild-eyed and dishevelled women in it. The men are lantern-jawed, with several days' growth of beard. Most of them carry rude weapons—staves, bill-hooks, crow-bars, and the like— and are in as excited a condition as the women. Some are bare-headed, others affect a kind of Phrygian cap. Cobblers predominate.

Enter Lorenzo de Medici *and* Cosimo de Medici. *They wear cloaks of scarlet brocade, and, to avoid notice, hold masks to their faces.*

Cos.

What purpose doth the foul and greasy plebs
Ensue to-day here?

Lor.

                        I nor know nor care.

Cos.

How thrall'd thou art to the philosophy
Of Epicurus! Naught that's human I
Deem alien from myself. [*To a* Cobbler.] Make
        answer, fellow!
What empty hope hath drawn thee by a thread
Forth from the *obs*cene hovel where thou starvest?

Cob.
No empty hope, your Honour, but the full
Assurance that to-day, as yesterday,
Savonarola will let loose his thunder
Against the vices of the idle rich
And from the brimming cornucopia
Of his immense vocabulary pour
Scorn on the lamentable heresies
Of the New Learning and on all the art
Later than Giotto.

Cos.
                    Mark how absolute
The knave is!

Lor.
                    Then are parrots rational
When they regurgitate the thing they hear!
This fool is but an unit of the crowd,
And crowds are senseless as the vasty deep
That sinks or surges as the moon dictates.
I know these crowds, and know that any man
That hath a glib tongue and a rolling eye
Can as he willeth with them.

> [*Removes his mask and mounts steps of Loggia.*]

                    Citizens!

> [*Prolonged yells and groans from the crowd.*]

Yes, I am he, I am that same Lorenzo
Whom you have nicknamed the Magnificent.

> [*Further terrific yells, shakings of fists, brandish-
> ings of bill-hooks, insistent cries of 'Death to*

Lorenzo!' 'Down with the Magnificent!' Cobblers
on fringe of crowd, down C., *exhibit especially all*
the symptoms of epilepsy, whooping-cough, and
other ailments.]

You love not me.

[*The crowd makes an ugly rush.* LOR. *appears*
likely to be dragged down and torn limb from limb,
but raises one hand in nick of time, and continues :]

Yet I deserve your love.

[*The yells are now variegated with dubious mur-*
murs. A cobbler down C. *thrusts his face feverishly*
in the face of another and repeats, in a hoarse
interrogative whisper, 'Deserves our love?']

Not for the sundry boons I have bestow'd
And benefactions I have lavishèd
Upon Firenze, City of the Flowers,
But for the love that in this rugged breast
I bear you.

[*The yells have now died away, and there is a sharp*
fall in dubious murmurs. The cobbler down C. *says,*
in an ear-piercing whisper, 'The love he bears
us', drops his lower jaw, nods his head repeatedly,
and awaits in an intolerable state of suspense the
orator's next words.]

I am not a blameless man,

[*Some dubious murmurs.*]

Yet for that I have lov'd you passing much,
Shall some things be forgiven me.

> [*Noises of cordial assent.*]

There dwells
In this our city, known unto you all,
A man more virtuous than I am, and
A thousand times more intellectual;
Yet envy not I him, for—shall I name him?—
He loves not you. His name? I will not cut
Your hearts by speaking it. Here let it stay
On tip o' tongue.

> [*Insistent clamour.*]

Then steel you to the shock!—
Savonarola.

> [*For a moment or so the crowd reels silently under
> the shock. Cobbler down* C. *is the first to recover
> himself and cry 'Death to Savonarola!' The cry
> instantly becomes general.* LOR. *holds up his hand
> and gradually imposes silence.*]

His twin bug-bears are
Yourselves and that New Learning which I hold
Less dear than only you.

> [*Profound sensation. Everybody whispers 'Than
> only you' to everybody else. A woman near steps
> of Loggia attempts to kiss hem of* LOR.'s *garment.*]

Would you but con

With me the old philosophers of Hellas,
Her fervent bards and calm historians,
You would arise and say 'We will not hear
Another word against them!'

> [*The crowd already says this, repeatedly, with
> great emphasis.*]

                Take the Dialogues
Of Plato, for example. You will find
A spirit far more truly Christian
In them than in the ravings of the sour-soul'd
Savonarola.

> [*Prolonged cries of 'Death to the Sour-Souled
> Savonarola!' Several cobblers detach themselves
> from the crowd and rush away to read the Platonic
> Dialogues. Enter* SAVONAROLA. *The crowd, as he
> makes his way through it, gives up all further
> control of its feelings, and makes a noise for which
> even the best zoologists might not find a good com-
> parison. The staves and bill-hooks wave like twigs
> in a storm. One would say that* SAV. *must have died
> a thousand deaths already. He is, however, un-
> harmed and unruffled as he reaches the upper step
> of the Loggia.* LOR. *meanwhile has rejoined* COS.
> *in the Piazza.*]

SAV.

        Pax vobiscum, brothers!

> [*This does but exacerbate the crowd's frenzy.*]

VOICE OF A COBBLER.
Hear his false lips cry Peace when there is no
Peace!

SAV.
          Are not you ashamed, O Florentines,

[*Renewed yells, but also some symptoms of manly
shame.*]

That hearken'd to Lorenzo and now reel
Inebriate with the exuberance
Of his verbosity?

[*The crowd makes an obvious effort to pull itself
together.*]

                    A man can fool
Some of the people all the time, and can
Fool all the people sometimes, but he cannot
Fool *all* the people *all* the time.

[*Loud cheers. Several cobblers clap one another on
the back. Cries of 'Death to Lorenzo!' The meeting is now well in hand.*]

                         To-day
I must adopt a somewhat novel course
In dealing with the awful wickedness
At present noticeable in this city.
I do so with reluctance. Hitherto
I have avoided personalities.
But now my sense of duty forces me
To a departure from my custom of

Naming no names. One name I must and shall
Name.

> [*All eyes are turned on* LOR., *who smiles un-
> comfortably.*]

No, I do not mean Lorenzo. He
Is 'neath contempt.

> [*Loud and prolonged laughter, accompanied with
> hideous grimaces at* LOR. *Exeunt* LOR. *and* COS.]

I name a woman's name,

> [*The women in the crowd eye one another sus-
> piciously.*]

A name known to you all—four-syllablèd,
Beginning with an L.

> [*Tense pause. Enter* LUC., *carrying the ring,
> and stands, unobserved by any one, on outskirt of
> crowd.* SAV. *utters the name:*]

Lucrezia!

LUC. [*With equal intensity.*]
Savonarola!

> [SAV. *starts violently and stares in direction of her
> voice.*]

Yes, I come, I come!

> [*Forces her way to steps of Loggia. The crowd is
> much bewildered, and the cries of 'Death to
> Lucrezia Borgia!' are few and sporadic.*]

Why didst thou call me?

[SAV. *looks somewhat embarrassed.*]

What is thy distress?
I see it all! The sanguinary mob
Clusters to rend thee! As the antler'd stag,
With fine eyes glazèd from the too-long chase,
Turns to defy the foam-fleck'd pack, and thinks,
In his last moment, of some graceful hind
Seen once afar upon a mountain-top,
E'en so, Savonarola, didst thou think,
In thy most dire extremity, of me.
And here I am! Courage! The horrid hounds
Droop tail at sight of me and fawn away
Innocuous.

[*The crowd does indeed seem to have fallen com-
pletely under the sway of* LUC.'S *magnetism, and
is evidently convinced that it had been about to
make an end of the monk.*]

Take thou, and wear henceforth,
As a sure talisman 'gainst future perils,
This little, little ring.

[SAV. *makes awkward gesture of refusal. Angry
murmurs from the crowd. Cries of 'Take thou the
ring!' 'Churl!' 'Put it on!' etc.*
    Enter the Borgias' FOOL *and stands unnoticed
on fringe of crowd.*]

I hoped you'ld like it—
Neat but not gaudy. Is my taste at fault?

I'd so look'd forward to—[Sob.] No, I'm not crying.
But just a little hurt.

> [Hardly a dry eye in the crowd. Also swayings and
> snarlings indicative that SAV.'s life is again not
> worth a moment's purchase. SAV. makes awkward
> gesture of acceptance, but just as he is about to put
> ring on finger, the FOOL touches his lute and
> sings :—]

> Wear not the ring
> It hath an unkind sting,
>   Ding, dong, ding.
> Bide a minute,
> There's poison in it,
>   Poison in it,
>   Ding-a-dong, dong, ding.

LUC.
    The fellow lies.

> [The crowd is torn with conflicting opinions.
> Mingled cries of 'Wear not the ring!' 'The fellow
> lies!' 'Bide a minute!' 'Death to the Fool!'
> 'Silence for the Fool!' 'Ding-a-dong, dong, ding!'
> etc.]

FOOL
        [Sings.]
> Wear not the ring,
> For Death's a robber-king,
>   Ding, [etc.]

There's no trinket
      Is what you think it,
      What you think it,
            Ding-a-dong, [*etc.*]

[SAV. *throws ring in* LUC.'s *face. Enter* POPE
JULIUS II, *with Papal army.*]

POPE
Arrest that man and woman!

[*Re-enter Guelfs and Ghibellines fighting.* SAV.
and LUC. *are arrested by Papal officers. Enter*
MICHAEL ANGELO. ANDREA DEL SARTO *appears
for a moment at a window.* PIPPA *passes. Brothers
of the Misericordia go by, singing a Requiem for
Francesca da Rimini. Enter* BOCCACCIO, BENVE-
NUTO CELLINI, *and many others, making remarks
highly characteristic of themselves but scarcely
audible through the terrific thunderstorm which
now bursts over Florence and is at its loudest and
darkest crisis as the Curtain falls.*]

ACT IV

TIME: *Three hours later.*
SCENE: *A Dungeon on the ground-floor of the Palazzo
    Civico.*

*The stage is bisected from top to bottom by a wall,
on one side of which is seen the interior of* LUCREZIA'S
cell, on the other that of SAVONAROLA'S.

*Neither he nor she knows that the other is in the next
cell. The audience, however, knows this.*

*Each cell (because of the width and height of the
proscenium) is of more than the average Florentine size,
but is bare even to the point of severity, its sole amenities
being some straw, a hunk of bread, and a stone pitcher.
The door of each is facing the audience. Dim-ish light.*

LUCREZIA *wears long and clanking chains on her
wrists, as does also* SAVONAROLA. *Imprisonment has left
its mark on both of them.* SAVONAROLA'S *hair has turned
white. His whole aspect is that of a very old, old man.*
LUCREZIA *looks no older than before, but has gone mad.*

SAV.
Alas, how long ago this morning seems
This evening! A thousand thousand æons
Are scarce the measure of the gulf betwixt
My then and now. Methinks I must have been
Here since the dim creation of the world
And never in that interval have seen
The tremulous hawthorn burgeon in the brake,
Nor heard the hum o' bees, nor woven chains
Of buttercups on Mount Fiesole
What time the sap lept in the cypresses,

Imbuing with the friskfulness of Spring
Those melancholy trees. I do forget
The aspect of the sun. Yet I was born
A freeman, and the Saints of Heaven smiled
Down on my crib. What would my sire have said,
And what my dam, had anybody told them
The time would come when I should occupy
A felon's cell? O the disgrace of it!—
The scandal, the incredible come-down!
It masters me. I see i' my mind's eye
The public prints—'Sharp Sentence on a Monk.'
What then? I thought I was of sterner stuff
Than is affrighted by what people think.
Yet thought I so because 'twas thought of me,
And so 'twas thought of me because I had
A hawk-like profile and a baleful eye.
Lo! my soul's chin recedes, soft to the touch
As half-churn'd butter. Seeming hawk is dove,
And dove's a gaol-bird now. Fie, out upon 't!

Luc.
How comes it? I am Empress Dowager
Of China—yet was never crown'd. This must
Be seen to.

> [*Quietly gathers some straw and weaves a crown,
> which she puts on.*]

Sav.
              O, what a degringolade!
The great career I had mapp'd out for me—
Nipp'd i' the bud. What life, when I come out,
Awaits me? Why, the very Novices
And callow Postulants will draw aside

As I pass by, and say 'That man hath done
Time!' And yet shall I wince? The worst of Time
Is not in having done it, but in doing 't.

LUC.
Ha, ha, ha, ha! Eleven billion pig-tails
Do tremble at my nod imperial,—
The which is as it should be.

SAV.

                I have heard
That gaolers oft are willing to carouse
With them they watch o'er, and do sink at last
Into a drunken sleep, and then's the time
To snatch the keys and make a bid for freedom.
Gaoler! Ho, Gaoler!

     [*Sounds of lock being turned and bolts withdrawn.
     Enter the Borgias'* FOOL, *in plain clothes, carry-
     ing bunch of keys.*]

                I have seen thy face
Before.

FOOL
       I saved thy life this afternoon, Sir.

SAV.
Thou art the Borgias' fool?

FOOL
                 Say rather, was.
Unfortunately I have been discharg'd
For my betrayal of Lucrezia,
So that I have to speak like other men—
Decasyllabically, and with sense.

An hour ago the gaoler of this dungeon
Died of an apoplexy. Hearing which,
I ask'd for and obtain'd his billet.

SAV.

                        Fetch
A stoup o' liquor for thyself and me.

                      [*Exit* GAOLER.]

Freedom! there's nothing that thy votaries
Grudge in the cause of thee. That decent man
Is doom'd by me to lose his place again
To-morrow morning when he wakes from out
His hoggish slumber. Yet I care not.

   [*Re-enter* GAOLER *with a leathern bottle and two
   glasses.*]

                        Ho!
This is the stuff to warm our vitals, this
The panacea for all mortal ills
And sure elixir of eternal youth.
Drink, bonniman!

   [GAOLER *drains a glass and shows signs of instant
   intoxication.* SAV. *claps him on shoulder and
   replenishes glass.* GAOLER *drinks again, lies down
   on floor, and snores.* SAV. *snatches the bunch of
   keys, laughs long but silently, and creeps out on tip-
   toe, leaving door ajar.*

    LUC. *meanwhile has lain down on the straw in
   her cell, and fallen asleep.*

    Noise of bolts being shot back, jangling of keys,
   grating of lock, and the door of LUC.'S cell flies
   open.* SAV. *takes two steps across the threshold,*

his arms outstretched and his upturned face trans-
figured with a great joy.]

How sweet the open air
Leaps to my nostrils! O the good brown earth
That yields once more to my elastic tread
And laves these feet with its remember'd dew!

[*Takes a few more steps, still looking upwards.*]

Free!—I am free! O naked arc of heaven,
Enspangled with innumerable—no,
Stars are not there. Yet neither are there clouds!
The thing looks like a ceiling! [*Gazes downward.*]
        And this thing
Looks like a floor. [*Gazes around.*] And that white
        bundle yonder
Looks curiously like Lucrezia.

[LUC. *awakes at sound of her name, and sits up
    sane.*]

There must be some mistake.

LUC. [*Rises to her feet.*]
                    There is indeed!
A pretty sort of prison I have come to,
In which a self-respecting lady's cell
Is treated as a lounge!

SAV.
                    I had no notion
You were in here. I thought I was out there.
I will explain—but first I'll make amends.
Here are the keys by which your durance ends.

The gate is somewhere in this corridor,
And so good-bye to this interior!

> [*Exeunt* SAV. *and* LUC. *Noise, a moment later,
> of a key grating in a lock, then of gate creaking on
> its hinges; triumphant laughs of fugitives; loud
> slamming of gate behind them.*
>
> *In* SAV.'S *cell the* GAOLER *starts in his sleep,
> turns his face to the wall, and snores more than
> ever deeply. Through open door comes a cloaked
> figure.*]

CLOAKED FIGURE
Sleep on, Savonarola, and awake
Not in this dungeon but in ruby Hell!

> [*Stabs* GAOLER, *whose snores cease abruptly.
> Enter* POPE JULIUS II, *with Papal retinue carry-
> ing torches.* MURDERER *steps quickly back into
> shadow.*]

POPE [*To body of* GAOLER.]
Savonarola, I am come to taunt
Thee in thy misery and dire abjection.
Rise, Sir, and hear me out.

MURD. [*Steps forward.*]
      Great Julius,
Waste not thy breath. Savonarola's dead.
I murder'd him.

POPE
     Thou hadst no right to do so.
Who art thou, pray?

MURD.

Cesare Borgia,
Lucrezia's brother, and I claim a brother's
Right to assassinate whatever man
Shall wantonly and in cold blood reject
Her timid offer of a poison'd ring.

POPE
Of this anon.

[*Stands over body of* GAOLER.]

Our present business
Is general woe. No nobler corse hath ever
Impress'd the ground. O, let the trumpets speak it!

[*Flourish of trumpets.*]

This was the noblest of the Florentines.
His character was flawless, and the world
Held not his parallel. O, bear him hence
With all such honours as our State can offer.
He shall interrèd be with noise of cannon,
As doth befit so militant a nature.
Prepare these obsequies.

[*Papal officers lift body of* GAOLER.]

A PAPAL OFFICER

But this is not
Savonarola. It is some one else.

CESARE
Lo! 'tis none other than the Fool that I
Hoof'd from my household but two hours agone.

I deem'd him no good riddance, for he had
The knack of setting tables on a roar.
What shadows we pursue! Good night, sweet Fool,
And flights of angels sing thee to thy rest!

POPE
Interrèd shall he be with signal pomp.
No honour is too great that we can pay him.
He leaves the world a vacuum. Meanwhile,
Go we in chase of the accursèd villain
That hath made escapado from this cell.
To horse! Away! We'll scour the country round
For Sav'narola till we hold him bound.
Then shall you see a cinder, not a man,
Beneath the lightnings of the Vatican!

> [*Flourish, alarums and excursions, flashes of
> Vatican lightning, roll of drums, etc. Through
> open door of cell is led in a large milk-white horse,
> which the* POPE *mounts as the Curtain falls.*]

Remember, please, before you formulate your impressions, that saying of Brown's: 'The thing *must* be judged as a whole.' I like to think that whatever may seem amiss to us in these four Acts of his would have been righted by collation with that Fifth which he did not live to achieve.

I like, too, to measure with my eyes the yawning gulf between stage and study. Very different from the message of cold print to our imagination are the messages of flesh and blood across footlights to our eyes and ears. In the warmth and brightness of a crowded theatre 'Savonarola' might, for aught one knows, seem perfect. 'Then why,' I hear my gentle readers asking, 'did you thrust the play on *us*, and, not on a theatrical manager?'

That question has a false assumption in it. In the course of the past eight years I have thrust 'Savonarola' on any number of theatrical managers. They have all of them been (to use the technical phrase) 'very kind.' All have seen great merits in the work; and if I added together all the various merits thus seen I should have no doubt that 'Savonarola' was the best play never produced. The point on which all the managers are unanimous is that they have no use for a play without an ending. This is why I have fallen back, at last, on gentle readers, whom now I hear asking why I did not, as Brown's literary executor, try to finish the play myself. Can they never ask a question without a false assumption in it? I did try, hard, to finish 'Savonarola.'

Artistically, of course, the making of such an attempt was indefensible. Humanly, not so. It is clear throughout the play—especially perhaps in Acts III and IV—that if Brown had not steadfastly in his mind the hope of production on the stage, he had nothing in his mind at all. Horrified though he would have been by the idea of letting me kill his Monk, he would rather have done even this than doom his play to everlasting unactedness. I took, therefore, my courage in both hands, and made out a scenario. . . .

Dawn on summit of Mount Fiesole. Outspread view of Florence (Duomo, Giotto's Tower, etc.) as seen from that eminence.—NICCOLO MACHIAVELLI, *asleep on grass, wakes as sun rises. Deplores his exile from Florence,* LORENZO'S *unappeasable hostility, etc. Wonders if he could not somehow secure the* POPE'S *favour. Very cynical. Breaks off :* But who are these that scale the mountain-side? | Savonarola and Lucrezia | Borgia!—*Enter through a trap-door, back* C. [*trap-door veiled from audience by a grassy ridge*], SAV. *and* LUC. *Both gasping and footsore from their climb.* [*Still with chains on their wrists? or not?*]— MACH. *steps unobserved behind a cypress and listens.*— SAV. *has a speech to the rising sun*—Th' effulgent hope that westers from the east | Daily. *Says that* his *hope, on the contrary, lies in escape* To that which easters not from out the west, | That fix'd abode of freedom which men call | America! *Very bitter against* POPE.— LUC. *says that she, for her part, means* To start afresh in that uncharted land. | Which austers not from out the antipod, | Australia!—*Exit* MACH., *unobserved, down trap-door behind ridge, to betray* LUC. *and* SAV.— *Several longish speeches by* SAV. *and* LUC. *Time is thus given for* MACH. *to get into touch with* POPE, *and time for* POPE *and retinue to reach the slope of Fiesole.* SAV., *glancing down across ridge, sees these sleuth-hounds, points them out to* LUC. *and cries* Bewray'd! LUC. By whom? SAV. I know not, but suspect | The hand of that sleek serpent Niccolo | Machiavelli.—SAV. *and* LUC. *rush down* C. *but find their way barred by the foot-lights.*—LUC. We will not be ta'en | Alive. And here availeth us my lore | In what pertains to poison. Yonder herb | [*points to a herb growing down* R.] Is deadly nightshade. Quick, Monk! Pluck we it!—

Sav. and Luc. die just as Pope appears over ridge, followed by retinue in full cry.—Pope's *annoyance at being foiled is quickly swept away on the great wave of Shakespearean chivalry and charity that again rises in him. He gives Sav. a funeral oration similar to the one meant for him in Act IV, but even more laudatory and more stricken. Of Luc., too, he enumerates the virtues, and hints that the whole terrestrial globe shall be hollowed to receive her bones. Ends by saying :* In deference to this our double sorrow Sun shall not shine to-day nor shine to-morrow.—*Sun drops quickly back behind eastern horizon, leaving a great darkness, on which the Curtain slowly falls.*

All this might be worse, yes. The skeleton passes muster. But in the attempt to incarnate and ensanguine it I failed wretchedly. I saw that Brown was, in comparison with me, a master. Thinking I might possibly fare better in his method of work than in my own, I threw the skeleton into a cupboard, sat down, and waited to see what Savonarola and those others would do.

They did absolutely nothing. I sat watching them, pen in hand, ready to record their slightest movement. Not a little finger did they raise. Yet I knew they must be alive. Brown had always told me they were quite independent of him. Absurd to suppose that by the accident of his own death they had ceased to breathe. . . . Now and then, overcome with weariness, I dozed at my desk, and whenever I woke I felt that these rigid creatures had been doing all sorts of wonderful things while my eyes were shut. I felt that they disliked me. I came to dislike them in return, and forbade them my room.

Some of you, my readers, might have better luck with them than I. Invite them, propitiate them, watch them! The writer of the best Fifth Act sent to me shall have his work tacked on to Brown's; and I suppose I could get him a free pass for the second night.

THE WORLD'S CLASSICS

THE WORLD'S CLASSICS